WINTER'S HEART

Suzanne Cass

S C

STORM CLOUD PRESS

Winter's Heart

Storm Cloud Press, Perth Australia

Copyright © 2025 by Suzanne Cass

Cover by Vikncharlie

All rights reserved.

ISBN: 9780648643067

To all my Swedish friends.

CHAPTER ONE

Nikki stopped walking, captivated by the beautiful vista of the frozen lake surrounded by snow-capped fir trees spread out in front of her. Despite her fluffy bathrobe, the freezing air chilled her skin, causing goosebumps to erupt across her body. Cold didn't begin to describe the temperature; it was well below freezing. Every frosty breath of air she drew into her lungs was painful, and she could feel the tip of her nose turning pink, even though the short walk between the house and the sauna at the bottom of the garden was only a hundred yards or so.

She took a few more steps, and pulled open the door to the little red wooden hut, plunging inside with a gasp of relief. The heat was a sudden, intense contrast to the cold outside, hitting her like a brick wall. Nikki had lit the stove in the tiny sauna an hour ago, to make sure the hut reached the correct temperature, and right now the little thermometer said 77C. Which was just about perfect.

Kicking off her fleece-lined boots, she hesitated a second before untying the knot on her robe. There was no one around for miles, but Nikki still glanced self-consciously out the window before slowly removing her garment and hanging it neatly on the hook at the back of the door, leaving her standing naked in the middle of the hut.

The Swedes were so open about taking a sauna nude, they'd grown up with it all their lives, it was part of their culture. But in the face of their nonchalance, she could admit how much of a prude she really was. In this isolated little house, she was completely alone, however, and so decided to give it a try. It was her last day here, so why not indulge herself?

Nikki was grateful no one else was around to pass judgment on her body. She'd always been slender, but with all the stress of her job over the past few months and her recent relationship breakup—Bradley's revelation that he was in love with someone else had broken something inside her, especially when he'd walked out and left as if she meant nothing to him—she was teetering on the edge of being too skinny. So skinny her hip bones were almost protruding through her jeans, and her arms had begun to appear skeletal. At least these ten days in the snowy wilderness where all there was to do was eat and read and take long walks through the forest had helped her gain back a few of those lost pounds.

Feeling decidedly empowered with her newfound shamelessness, Nikki used a cute wooden cup to pour water over the hot stones on top of the stove and settled herself down onto the carefully folded towel she'd placed on the bench seat earlier. With a sigh, she pinned her long hair into a loose knot, leaned her head back against the wooden wall, closed her eyes, and let the hot steam envelop her. Why had it taken her so long to discover the appeal of a sauna? So good for the skin, so good for her mental health as well. Relaxation wasn't something that came easily to Nikki, but the heat of the sauna definitely helped to burn away some of that built-in stress. She was still working up to the idea of a roll in the snow or an ice plunge afterwards. The well-documented health benefits of cold therapy couldn't outweigh her abhorrence of icy water, not in her mind anyway.

After luxuriating in the steam for a few moments, she opened her eyes so she could stare out the window. Could this place be any more beautiful and serene? She'd be thanking Tammy for recommending this little holiday hut as a getaway after the intense few weeks they'd spent working together almost night and day. Lost in the wilds of the Swedish forests, she couldn't have picked a more perfect place. It was midwinter, and this far north, the sun merely skimmed the horizon instead of rising properly, turning the sky wonderful pale mauves and oranges, colors she'd love to capture in a painting, if only she were an artist. It would be dark by mid-afternoon, but Nikki didn't mind; it gave her an excuse to curl up on the couch and read another of the many books she'd found in the well-stocked library.

A prickle of awareness ran through her and the nice relaxing buzz she had going vanished in a flash. Why did she feel as if someone was watching her? No one else was out here, she was utterly alone. She leaned forward warily and turned her head to peer out the side window. A flicker of movement caught her eye, but by the time she'd turned to face the entrance, standing up in alarm, the door to the sauna swung open, letting in a rush of freezing air.

A man stood at the entrance, blocking the exit with his large bulk. She screamed and tried to cover her nakedness. "What the—"

"Are you Dr. Nikita Winter?" the man demanded in a harsh voice, cutting her off.

"Get out," she screamed, wanting to grab her robe, but it was on the door behind him. "Get out!" she yelled again, cowering backward, crossing her arms over her breasts. But there was nowhere for her to go, his large, male body nearly overwhelmed the tiny hut. Did this man mean to hurt her?

Her whole body shook, not only from the arctic air blasting in, but from pure fear.

"Sorry, ma'am, I can't do that." He avoided looking at her naked body as he removed her robe and offered it to her. She was too dumbfounded to take it, and continued to gape at him, cringing like a cornered animal. "Put this on," he demanded when she didn't move.

Dazed, she stared at him, her mind refusing to function. Where had he come from? He couldn't have driven here; the hut was completely cut off by snow. The owner had brought her in using his snowmobile and was going to pick her up and take her back to town the same way.

Who was he? In her blind panicked state, she sketched a tall figure, dressed in white—down to his white knit cap and white boots—square-jawed with a rough growth that wasn't quite long enough to be called a beard, a long, hawk-like nose with penetrating hazel eyes that were zeroed in on her. He looked like one of those commandos you saw in the movies, except all in white instead of black. It dawned on her slowly. White, so he could hide in the snow. Oh, God, what was going on here? He must be here to murder her. Afterward, he'd vanish back into the snowy landscape as if he'd never existed, and no one would be any the wiser. The owner would find her body tomorrow when he came to collect her, but it would all be too late by then.

A low moan leached from her throat.

The man gave a grunt of annoyance and pushed the robe toward her. "Put this on," he said again. "I will not hurt you. Please put it on."

It took the man physically pushing the garment into her hands for her body to function again. Quickly, she scrambled to pull the clothing on. At least if she was going to die, she would not do it buck naked. He watched her slip the robe over her shoulders and cinch it around her waist, his sharp gaze never leaving her face, never even once flickering below her chin. It took her a few seconds to realize that he was staring at her steadily, not leering at her. Now that she thought about it, he'd had plenty of opportunity to ogle her if he'd wanted to, but he wasn't. In fact, his face remained impassive. And he hadn't moved any closer, merely stayed in the doorway. If he intended to rape and murder her, then surely he would've taken advantage of her nudity? Used the surprise of his sudden appearance to his advantage and overpowered her. But he remained standing there, unruffled and solid as a rock.

Her heart still felt like it was going to leap out of her chest, but she finally stopped being so frightened that she couldn't think straight. She needed to come up with a way out of this predicament. What was it her grandmother used to say to her? Never let them see your fear. Go down kicking and screaming if you have to, but don't let them see your fear. Nikki's grandmother had been a strong woman who'd lived an eventful life and had been the catalyst for Nikki's choice of profession. She drew in a deep breath and stood taller, trying to channel the ghost of her grandmother, drawing in strength with every breath.

He gave a nod of approval now she was dressed. "I'm sorry, I didn't mean to scare you," he said in that calm, authoritative voice. "But I need to confirm that you are Nikita Winter."

Bitterly cold air seeped in through the open door, but his large body filled the entrance, effectively trapping her. Numerous escape plans circled her head, but short of shoving him backward out into the snow—which would require her to take him by surprise, and that wasn't going to happen—she could see no way out. If only she knew some martial arts or had taken a women's defense class, then perhaps she might've considered a bid for freedom. Although she highly doubted she could outrun him wearing nothing more than a bathrobe and bare feet to run through the thigh-deep snow.

"Ma'am," he said roughly, snapping her out of her reverie. "Please answer my question."

She could see no other option, so she drew in a breath and tightened the sash around her waist, raising her chin to look him in the eye. "Yes, I'm Nikki. Who's asking?"

A muscle twitched in the man's cheek, the only sign Nikki could see that he was relieved by her admission. "I'm Jáhkot Utsi. A police inspector with the Svensk Polis. I'm here to protect you," he replied.

A police officer? Should she believe him? What was a cop doing all the way out here? As if reading her mind, he pulled a badge from some hidden pocket and flashed it for her to see. It looked real enough. But the whole scenario was just so surreal. All she'd wanted was to enjoy a lovely sauna and take in the stunning view. There was no imaginable situation she could come up with that allowed for a police officer dressed in camouflage white to come bursting through her door and demand he was here to safeguard her. It was preposterous. This had to be a joke, right?

"Protect me from what?" she asked, not hiding her mocking tone. She didn't need protection. She was a marine scientist on a short holiday after weeks of conducting a thorough investigation in the nearby fjords of Norway. A normal person, with no enemies to speak of, carrying on with her normal life; she certainly wasn't in any danger. The initial shock and adrenaline of this policeman's appearance was wearing off, making her fingers shake and her fear turn to irritation.

"Here, put these on. We need to get you out of here as soon as possible." He shoved her boots toward her, ignoring her question. His impatience shimmered around him, almost like a visible aura. She put her feet into the boots slowly, taking her time, delaying as best she could, watching his eyes dart to the left and then to the right, while the rest of his body remained as still as a statue. "I'll fill you in on all the details later, but for now, we need to move. Quick, go to the house," he added when he noticed her stalling, moving out of the doorway and gesturing for her to go ahead.

Some of his agitation was rubbing off on her and while she didn't believe there was any danger, she did as she was told, but at a dignified walk rather than a run. The police officer—what had he said his name was, Jáhkot?—followed her up the path, his gaze continuously raking the surroundings, so alert he reminded her of a German Shepherd on point. Walking through the fresh snow made it slow going, so she followed the footsteps she'd made on the way down to the sauna, which meant that Jáhkot was practically breathing down her neck by the time she laid her fingers on the door handle of the cottage. She was surprised he hadn't picked her up and thrown her over his shoulder, he was so hyper. Stepping inside, she had a sudden impulse to slam the door in his face. He beat her to it, however, pushing her over the threshold and shutting the door firmly behind him, glancing once more outside as he did so.

Only then did she notice the gun. She hadn't seen it when he'd burst into the sauna, but he had one in his hand now, pointed at the floor.

The sight of the gun pushed her over the edge. There were limits to what a normal person could put up with, and she'd had about enough of this nonsense.

"How dare you," she said, putting her hands on her hips as she rounded on him, hoping to hide the fact they were still shaking. "How dare you come here and scare the shit out of me, and act as if we've been dropped into some terrible B-grade movie? I'm not moving from this spot until you tell me exactly what's going on." Nikki was proud of herself. Look at her, channeling her grandmother and standing up to this guy. Yes, he might be a police officer—although that was still debatable—but he had no right to order her around like this. Not without a bloody good explanation. It was out of character; she normally hated confrontation, but this was like no other situation she'd ever found herself in. A scientist by profession as well as by nature, she was always coolheaded, liked things that were logical and relatable. She hated to be rushed or do anything in a perfunctory manner. She was all about digging down to find the sense of things. And in her world, this man made no sense at all.

Those intense, tawny eyes were trained on her again. "I'm sorry, ma'am, I'm not—"

She sliced through his explanation. "Nikki. My name is Nikki, not ma'am, or Nikita. That's what my mother calls me."

He gave a soft snort, and if she hadn't known better, she might've thought he was amused. His gaze softened. Holding up his gloved hand, he made a noise as if he were gentling a frisky horse. Which only incensed her more. She wasn't here for his amusement; she was deadly serious and she narrowed her eyes at him.

"Now… Nikki, I know this must be frightening for you," he said, hand still in the air.

"Damn right it is," she countered hotly, pulling the robe tighter around her body.

"And I'm sorry I don't have all the answers. My brief is to extract you to somewhere safe, and that's what I plan to do."

"Well, Jáhkot…" she stumbled over the name, not sure of the Swedish pronunciation.

"Call me Jacob," he said. "Only my mother calls me Jáhkot," he added with a cheeky tilt to his lips. Was he making a joke at her expense? And was that a hint of a dimple hidden in that smile? Forgetting herself for a second, she stared at him. Oh god, what a smile. It transformed his face. Made it almost beautiful, lighting up his eyes. If this had been any other situation, Nikki would've been transfixed.

Instead, she corralled her thoughts and sifted through her options. What could be so urgent that she had to leave right now? It was possible his supervisors, or whoever had sent him, had got it wrong. She wasn't in any immediate danger. This place was miles from anywhere. What could possibly be a threat to her out here? That thought made her wonder again how the officer had arrived, because there was no sign of any vehicle, but she put that thought out of her mind for now because there were more urgent questions needing answers.

Deciding she would reason with him, she said, "Ok. Look, Jacob, I'm leaving tomorrow, anyway. I'm supposed to meet up with my colleagues back in Bodø across the border in Norway. Can it wait until then?" There, she had a logical solution to his problem. The owner of this wonderful hut, Andreas, was due to come and pick her up at nine a.m. tomorrow morning and take her to her hire car in the nearby town of Jokkmokk. Then she would make the six-hour drive back into Norway to rendezvous with Tammy and Antoine and they would board the little charter flight to take them down to Oslo, and then onto a commercial flight back to the US. It was already arranged. Tammy and Antoine had also been taking a well-earned break, but they'd decided to travel farther north to tour the maze of fjords at the top end of Norway.

"No," he replied flatly. "It can't. You must get dressed in as warm clothing as you can find. After that, we'll—"

She stamped her foot. The man wasn't listening. If he wanted her to go right now, then he needed to give her a very good reason to move, otherwise she was staying put.

"Perhaps we can call someone to sort out this mess. Your supervisor maybe?" she asked scathingly. Andreas had given her a satellite phone to use in case of emergency, but until now she'd never even turned it on. "I'm sure my co-workers will vouch for—"

Jacob's face hardened. "I'm sorry to have to be the bearer of bad news, but both your co-workers are dead."

What? What had he just said?

"I'm telling you this, because we think you might be next on the killer's hit list," he added. "That's why we need to get moving. You're in danger here," his gaze flicked to the windows, not looking at her now.

Nikki's legs felt rubbery, no longer able to hold her weight. A foggy haze settled over her vision, and everything became blurry. That couldn't be true. Tammy and Antoine dead? No. No...

She crumpled to the ground with a soft thud.

CHAPTER TWO

Jacob dived to catch the woman before she hit the floor, but he could only grab wildly at thin air as she collapsed unceremoniously into a heap. Landing on his knees beside her, he saw that the thick, woolen rug, rather than the hard, wooden floor, had broken her fall. Nikki's eyes remained closed, and she was unresponsive. She'd fainted because he'd been unable to come up with an easy way to tell her the truth. God, he was a dick. He pulled one glove off to check her vitals, keeping his gun ready at his side in the other. Relief flooded him when he felt a strong pulse at her neck.

For one horrible second, he was taken back in time to a week prior, where he'd been in exactly the same position, down on his knees beside the man he should have been protecting. Crimson blood spurted from a gaping wound in Tristan's neck, even as Jacob had tried in vain to stem the bleeding with his hands. The man had died right there in front of him; he could do nothing to save him.

Jacob shook his head to rid himself of the image. It wouldn't help anyone if he allowed himself to spiral into the depths of his own incompetence. Besides, this woman was alive; she had a strong and vibrant pulse beneath his touch— she was merely unconscious. Thanks to his insensitivity.

He hated that he'd had to tell her the truth. But they needed to get moving, and it seemed like his only option, otherwise she would simply stand there and argue with him all day. He hadn't expected such a sudden and silent reaction to his words, however, and he mentally berated himself for being such an ass.

Mårten would've had some choice words for Jacob at his complete lack of empathy. Mårten was the good cop in their partnership, the one who kept a cool head, always easygoing, while Jacob was the reckless one. It was why they made such a good team. At least they had until they'd both dropped the ball in Malmo and let Tristan die. Now, depending on the outcome of the investigation, they might never work together again. He wished his partner was here right now; he'd handle this woman with much more compassion, while getting her to do exactly what he wanted—without making her faint. But Mårten was on enforced leave, the same as Jacob, only in Stockholm visiting his family, so Jacob would just have to suck it up and figure this out on his own.

As he leaned over her, he noticed her robe had gaped open at the front, revealing small, pert breasts. The same ones he'd so valiantly forced himself to avert his gaze from when he'd burst into the sauna and found her naked. This time his eyes caught and stayed fixed on all that creamy skin and rosy nipples, puckered with the cold. A soft fall of long, blonde hair fanned out around her head on the floor like a halo, her face so bewitching she reminded him of a fallen angel. In the sauna he'd catalogued the fact she was a good-looking woman, but that was as far as he'd allowed his mind to go; he had a job to do and just because she was decidedly attractive meant nothing. This woman's life was in danger, and he was the only one who could help her. Her life, and possibly his too, rested on his ability to protect her. And now look what he'd done. The last thing he needed was an unconscious subject, and him daydreaming over how attractive she was, while he wasted precious time. He was determined no one else would die on his watch. He had to get this right.

Tearing his gaze away from her chest, he patted her cheek with his free hand. "Dr. Winter, you need to wake up." She gave a small groan, but didn't rouse. He shook her shoulder gently. "Dr. Winter," he said, louder this time. "You need to wake up." Her pretty, pink lips pursed, and she murmured something incoherent, but her eyes remained stubbornly shut. She had amazing lips, full and luscious, tipped slightly up at the corners. Highly appealing and very, very kissable.

Concentrate, Jacob. He needed to stop thinking with his dick. This had never happened before; when he was on a mission, he was always completely focussed on the outcome. Not once had he ever allowed himself to be sidetracked by a girl, no matter how gorgeous she might be. "Nikki. Come on, wake up. Nikki." He shook her again, this time with intent, hoping the use of her first name might get through to her.

At last her eyelids fluttered open, and she stared at him with the bluest eyes he'd ever seen. They widened at the sight of him hovering over her and she sat up, flinching away from him, tugging her robe together. The dazed expression left her face as she took in her surroundings and then looked back at him with growing horror as she remembered his words. She shuffled across the floor on her hands and knees away from him, her eyes glazing over with tears.

"Did you say Tammy and Antoine are dead?" she whispered, sitting back on her haunches.

"I'm sorry, Nikki." He nodded slowly, watching her bottom lip tremble at his words. That fascinating mouth puckered, and a tear tracked down her cheek. God, he *was* an ass, but he had to do what he had to do. Hardening his resolve, said, "We have to get moving. Like I said, you are in imminent danger." He emphasized the last two words, praying his rough tone was enough to break through her grief and shock and get her moving.

Even though his orders had come from up high, they'd been light on actual details. The call had come through on his satellite phone an hour earlier. That phone was only used for emergencies and he was already on alert before he'd even picked it up. He should be on suspension—taking a leave of absence was the official term—while they investigated the reasons Jacob and Mårten's last mission had failed so spectacularly, so the call proved most unexpected. Even more unexpected, the voice on the other end had belonged to Biträdande Poliskommissarie Runar Staaf, the northern regional head of police, and a chill had run down his spine when he'd recognized his boss's boss. Jacob had only met Runar four or five times over the course of his career, and Jacob would not be his favorite person right now, not when he'd just let a witness die while in his custody. So, if the deputy commissioner had taken it upon himself to contact Jacob, then it must be damn important. Important enough to override his current suspension and bring him back online, even if it was under strict instructions to get this done as quickly as possible and not stray from his directive. Which was why he'd hightailed it here, running through the snow and ice for two miles to get to this woman, aware he may already be too late. His relief when he'd opened the door to the sauna and found her was immense, but that was only the start of his assignment. Now he had to convey her to his hut, then keep her safe until he received further orders.

"Let me help you up," he said, curbing his impatience and taking her arm.

"Leave me alone." She snatched her hand away, but not before he felt the slight tremors running through her. She was afraid. Of him, or of her predicament, he wasn't sure. Right now, it didn't matter, he just needed her to get moving. "I can do it myself." Nikki struggled to stand, yanking her robe more tightly around herself and swiping at the tears on her cheeks.

"You need to dress warmly. Hat, gloves, boots, thick jacket. We'll be walking through the snow," he said, taking a few steps closer, herding her toward the door he presumed led to a bedroom. "As quickly as you can," he added, as she backed away, those big blue eyes still wide with fear and anguish.

She turned and fled into the bedroom, shutting the door behind her, and he prowled around the small house, stopping at each window to examine the surrounding countryside. Looking for what, he wasn't sure. All he knew was there was a threat to Nikki's life. Two people had died, and they felt sure she was going to be next. Something to do with a recent project she'd been working on with her colleagues. Jacob didn't know whether he sought a lone sniper, a gang of thugs, or someone in between. If he could get her out of here and safely back to his hut, then hopefully he would throw whoever was hunting her off the scent.

This was the first time he'd been inside this little holiday house. Of course, he knew of its existence, had seen it on one of his many hikes from the other side of the lake. Knew that it belonged to Andreas Eriksson, who lived in Jokkmokk ten miles away, and rented it out on Airbnb. It was a traditional Swedish house, the wooden exterior painted red, the rustic interior decorated in pine and pale colors. Small but functional, with one large main room including a kitchenette, a single bedroom with ensuite to the side, and a wood-fired stove for heating. Which Nikki had stoked up well. So well, he was now sweating profusely inside his snow outfit.

It mirrored his own hut, the only other habitation within miles in this isolated little nook of the country. And the sole reason he'd been called in from his involuntary holiday to rescue this lady. Jacob grunted at the irony of it all. He and

Mårten had been forced to take a paid leave of absence after their last mission had ended in tragedy while the details were investigated. Jacob had chosen to go to his family's winter hut, a completely off-grid location, where he could unwind by getting back to nature and reconnect with his family traditions. But only two short days into his leave, the call had come in. He'd like to bet that it grated on the deputy commissioner to have to call him for a favor, when Jacob was so decidedly out of favor right now.

He continued to scour the countryside through the windows, but nothing moved, nothing seemed amiss. The pristine white blanket of snow remained unmarked. He would be able to see if anyone approached; their footprints would've announced them already. And he'd be able to spot an assailant before they got anywhere near the house, as the building sat in the middle of a large, cleared field with the lake to the right, forming another natural barrier. But he continued to stare out the windows, jumping at every whisper of wind in the eves and every flicker of a leaf on a branch. He was as jumpy as a cat on a hotplate. He needed to stop second-guessing himself and just keep reminding himself he was damn good at his job. Last week had been an unprecedented situation, and he would never allow himself to become distracted like that again. *Yeah, keep telling yourself that*, a small voice mocked him silently. *Fann*. He hated that traitorous voice.

After many long minutes, so long that Jacob was about to go up and rap on her door, Nikki emerged from the bedroom. Her eyes were red from more unshed tears and her face was pale and drawn, but there was resolve in the lines around her mouth. He was pleasantly surprised to see she'd dressed appropriately in hiking boots, blue waterproof pants, a thick yellow jacket, warm gloves, and a hot pink knit hat to finish the outfit. He couldn't help the grimace that flashed across his features, however. She'd stand out like a beacon with all that bright clothing against the white terrain. He couldn't help it. If only he'd thought to bring his spare snow camo outfit for her to wear. He'd have to take extra care on the trek back to his hut.

"What?" she demanded, seeing his look of consternation.

"Nothing." It'd do no good to scare her any more than she already was. He was usually an excellent judge of character, and while on the outside she'd reacted badly to his news of her friends' deaths, he sensed a core of steel inside this woman. Closing the distance so that he stood directly in front of her, he waited until she was looking at him. "My hut is about two miles from here. We're going to hike through the forest to get there. It should take us around an hour and a half." He'd completed the journey in less than forty-five minutes, but he needed to allow for the fact she was a civilian, unused to hiking through the snow and these intense cold temperatures. "I want you to do exactly as I say. Okay?"

"What? Don't you have a snowmobile or something?" She stared at him incredulously, completely ignoring his request for her cooperation. "You tell me I'm in immediate danger, but then you expect me to walk out of here?"

"Yes, I have transport. Back at my hut. That's why we're headed there," he explained. The terrain was too rough and the forest too thick to have ridden his snowmobile through it. He'd had to run cross country to get here, and planned on retracing his path to get back. The only problem was that whoever was after Nikki might also follow their trail. Again, there was nothing he could do about it. While he was capable of traveling through snowy terrain leaving the barest of traces, he hadn't been careful this time; the urgency of his mission overriding everything else, and now they might very well pay the price.

She puckered her lips in displeasure but, to his great

surprise, decided not to argue with him this time.

"So, will you do exactly as I tell you? Your life may depend on it," he reiterated. He had his doubts that she'd comply. In the few minutes he'd known her, she'd been nothing but stubborn and argumentative.

She glared at him but nodded slowly in reply, and he hoped she meant it. "Right. Stay close behind me. Do everything that I do. Step in my footsteps when you can." He led the way to the back door, bending down and squinting through the glass window to check they were still alone, expecting her to be right at his heels. Instead, when he turned his head, she was nowhere to be seen. *Va' fan?* They hadn't even left the safety of the house yet, and she'd already disobeyed him.

He stood up straight. Where was she? He broke out in a cold sweat. That was exactly what Tristan had done. Disobeyed a direct order to stay put. And he'd ended up dead.

A second later, she emerged from her bedroom, slinging a backpack over her shoulder. "I couldn't leave my computer," she said, ignoring the murderous look he sent her way. "My life is in here. All my work. I can't lose it."

This woman was going to be the death of him. Of them both. She came and stood behind him, calm as could be, and cocked one eyebrow when he continued to stare at her. "Are we going, or what?"

Tamping down his rising irritation, Jacob opened the door slowly and peered outside. When he was sure everything was clear, he beckoned for her to follow him down the steps and back along the pathway that led to the sauna. This way, they avoided making fresh tracks away from the house that would be easily spotted. Once past the front of the sauna, he veered to the right and into a small copse of birch trees, happy to see Nikki finally sticking to him like glue. Anyone who made the journey down to the small sauna would probably see their tracks leading off around the edge of the lake. All he could do now was get her back to his hut as quickly as possible and hope they weren't discovered too soon.

He did wonder about this undefined threat to Nikki's life. So far, he'd hadn't seen or heard anything that might suggest someone was watching, or that anyone was even in the vicinity. It didn't mean they weren't coming, however, and he should just be grateful they were getting out of the hut without incident.

For the next few minutes, the only sound was the crunch of snow beneath their boots and her breathing, which got heavier the farther they went as he navigated around the edge of the frozen lake, setting a pace he hoped she could keep up with. But she didn't complain or ask him to slow down, and true to her word, stuck to his heels, never once veering from his footsteps.

"Are you okay?" he asked, risking a quick glance behind to see how she was doing.

"I'm fine," she replied, puffing hard. "But it might pay you to remember your legs are longer than mine." It was only then that he realized she found it difficult to stay in his footsteps, having to stretch her legs considerably to make sure her gait matched his. No wonder she was out of breath. Without slowing down, he altered the length of his stride, taking shorter, sharper steps.

"Thank you," she muttered. "That's better."

Good. Her cooperation meant he had one less thing to worry about. As long as she stayed right behind him, he could keep her safe. Casting his awareness out into the snowy forest, he used all his senses to make sure they were alone. His Sámi heritage stood him in good stead when it came to moving through the forest. Growing up with family who still lived and worked in the traditional ways meant that he'd been hunting moose by the age of nine, tending herds of reindeer and driving dog sleds when he turned ten.

Thirty minutes later, they were deep in the forest, trudging through snow drifts beneath low overhanging branches of evergreen needles. The pine trees closed in on all sides, blocking most of the dying sunshine, which would be gone in the next half an hour.

He glanced behind to see how Nikki was going. She had her head down, making sure she matched her steps with his, and didn't look up until he came to a complete stop. "How are you going now?" he asked. He swung a small backpack off one shoulder and pulled out a water bottle, offering her a drink.

"I'm fine," she snapped, taking the bottle from him and gulping water in greedy sips. "You concentrate on not getting us lost, and I promise I'll keep up with you," she said, handing the water back. He noted that her breathing was accelerated, but not labored; much the same as his own. She was clearly fit, then. Those long, slender limbs he'd noted while she had been naked in the sauna hid muscular thighs beneath the soft skin.

"Can you go any faster?" he asked. "The sun is setting soon," he added.

"I'm a field scientist," she replied. "I hike up mountains and along beaches for a living." When he stared at her blankly, she added. "Yes, I can keep up."

Choosing to forego concealment for speed, he made a choice. "Stay as close to me as you can, but you can make your own path, if that's easier for you."

"Oh, gee, thanks."

They made it back to his hut forty-five minutes later, just as the dark engulfed the land, and he was nothing less than impressed by the woman behind him. True to her word, she'd kept up with his punishing pace without even a grumble. But as he opened the front door and ushered her in, she stumbled over the threshold and stood in the small mudroom panting and he knew she was just about done in. He took one last penetrating look outside before he locked the door securely behind him and let out a gust of breath. Safe. For now, at least. He felt better about this mission every minute, his confidence returning slowly. This wasn't the same as last week; the situation was completely different. Jacob stood on his own turf now, not in an unfamiliar city where snipers hid around every corner. He knew this country like the back of his hand, understood this land and her changing moods.

"You did great," he told her, reaching a hand out to steady her shoulder as she swayed a little. She merely flicked her blue gaze at him, hands hanging limply at her side, the normal acerbic comment missing. Her face was pale, and she shivered. They both needed to get warm before hypothermia became a problem. Even encased in warm hiking boots and a waterproof jacket, the temperature outside was glacial, and that was before the sun had set, when it'd plummeted even more. It must be at least 20C below out there. He was acclimatized, but she was a tourist, not used to these freezing temperatures. Jacob had banked the fire in the little pot-belly stove and brought in a pile of wood before he left, so the hut should be warm, and he could get it roaring soon enough.

"Here, let me help you." Slotting his gun in the shoulder holster he wore over his camo suit, he tugged off his gloves and dropped them on the floor, then helped to remove hers as well, reaching up and drawing down the zipper of her jacket. She watched him, letting him handle her like she was a shop store dummy, exhaustion evident on her face. But when he came to removing her backpack so he could slide the jacket down her arms, she snatched the bag away from him, giving him the hairy eyeball, as if she thought he might've been about to steal it.

"Are we safe now? Can I finally sit down?" she asked, voice rasping from exertion once he'd hung her jacket on a hook behind her. They weren't out of harm's way yet, not by a long shot, but being back in his hut gave him comfort nonetheless. This was his home ground, and he knew it like the back of his hand. If anything happened, he was prepared for it here.

"For now," he replied softly. "Come, sit down." He pointed at the small pine bench built into the wall. "I'll help you off with your boots." He crouched down in front of her.

"My feet are cold," she admitted, as he undid her laces. "Actually, they've been numb for the past half an hour." He wasn't really surprised, his were like frozen lumps, even inside his fur-lined Gore-Tex boots. "And my hands, too," she added with a grimace.

He looked down and saw her fingers were bright red, resting stiffly in her lap. *Faan*, she was showing early signs of frostbite. Resisting the urge to grab her hands and chafe them together—the worst thing you could do if you suspected frostbite—he sandwiched them carefully between his to warm them. Small and vulnerable inside his larger, calloused ones, he was surprised to feel a surge of... what... protectiveness? Which was absurd; he'd only just met the woman. She was right, though; they were like icicles. He needed to get them warm and soon.

Standing up, he stripped his own snowsuit off and left it in a white puddle of fabric on the floor, kicking off his boots as well. Underneath, he wore thick, thermal, woolen leggings and a dark-blue fleece shirt. Getting to his knees again, he lifted his shirt and gently took both her hands, placing them on his chest, flinching as her icy skin touched his. She gasped and tried to draw away, but he held her firm and looked her straight in the eyes.

"It's the best way to get them warm," he chided softly.

"But I… but you…" Her blue eyes widened, and her fingers tensed against the wall of his pecs. Even though they were the temperature of an ice block, Jacob was still acutely aware of her fingertips, his skin crackling with an energy he'd never felt before, and he stilled beneath her touch.

He'd slept with many women over the years and even managed a couple of longer-term relationships. His current lover, Freya, possessed considerable skills in the bedroom, and he'd enjoyed many an erotic night between the sheets. But not once in any of his encounters with any of the women he'd been with had it ever felt as if they were burning a brand into his skin. He wondered if Nikki was aware of it too. Perhaps she was, because her gaze never left his, her bow lips slightly parted as if in question.

Tearing his gaze away, he covered the backs of her hands with his shirt, and said, "It's okay. I'm used to the cold. Now let me get your boots off. Can you lift your foot into my lap?"

"Hmm?" She seemed a little dazed, so he leaned down as far as he could without dislodging her hands from his chest and grabbed her ankle, then lifted her boot into his lap to pull it off. Her foot was dry, which was a good start, but when he gently peeled back her sock, he saw that her little toe was completely white and waxy, with the rest swollen and red. Not good. Not good at all. This needed more than just his chest to warm them up. If he didn't do something soon, she might even lose that pinky toe. He silently reproached himself for failing to check her boots before their ninety-minute hike in freezing temperatures. Back at her hut, there'd been no time, and he'd had no choice but to force her outside in sub-standard clothing. And she'd gone, not making the slightest fuss, not asking him to stop even once. He glanced back up at her, deciding she was made of much tougher stuff than he'd given her credit for.

CHAPTER THREE

Jacob had gone very quiet as he kneeled before Nikki, studying her bare feet. She was feeling slightly bewildered. The trek through the freezing temperatures had made her movements slower and her thoughts more labored. But it wasn't the cold that'd shocked her into speechlessness just now; it was the jolt of having her palms pressed against Jacob's warm skin. Right on top of his pecs. His very firm, very muscular pecs. If only her hands weren't quite so lacking in feeling, she might even enjoy the sensation, be able to luxuriate in the soft curl of his chest hair beneath her fingers. Perhaps she could run her hands over the curve of his broad shoulders underneath his shirt, feel the flex of his well-built arms as he…

Nikki caught herself before her thoughts could go any farther. This man was a stranger. Admittedly, a handsome stranger with intense hazel eyes, determined to protect her, but there was no way she should be fantasizing about him or his chest hair. Or his arms. Her mind was muddled by the cold; she must have hypothermia.

Before she could properly process that thought, he suddenly scooped her off the bench, and she was in those muscular arms as she blinked in bewilderment, her backpack still clutched in her arms.

"What are you doing?" she demanded when she finally found her voice. He didn't answer, his mouth a grim line of determination. Had she done something wrong? Had he somehow read her mind and found her indecent thoughts disgusting? Gosh, the poor man was probably married, with a wife and children, and here she was fantasizing about touching him. He wasn't wearing a wedding band, but that didn't mean much nowadays. Searching his face for answers, she couldn't tell if he was angry or merely intent on getting her inside. Perhaps a little of both.

Using his shoulder, Jacob pushed through the door from the mudroom and into the main living area. Blessed warmth enveloped her, and she let out a sigh of relief. The mudroom had been warm compared to outside, but in here it was even more cozy. He placed her gently down on one of the four chairs surrounding a small, round table near a kitchenette. "Wait here a second. I'm going to get the fire going again," he instructed.

She did as she was told. Mainly because she wasn't sure she'd be able to stand, her feet were like leaden weights on the end of her legs. Frozen leaden weights. Placing her backpack on the floor next to her with clumsy fingers still numb from the cold, she watched Jacob move around the hut, putting wood from a stack next to the door into a slow combustion stove, then blowing on the embers to get it blazing again. He was all calm efficiency, but he also radiated a reined-in power, which intrigued her. She could barely keep her eyes from tracing the solid curves of his upper chest and shoulders that were clearly defined now by his body-hugging thermals. A very nice specimen of a man indeed. He moved as though he were at home in this little hut, and she wondered at his connection to it. It looked old, with traditional carvings in the beams above the doors, and the wooden floors beneath the animal skin rugs scarred and worn by the passage of many feet.

Jacob busied himself at the small kitchenette bench, running some water into a sink, and Nikki was finally reminded of her own nagging physical needs as her body slowly came back to life. She couldn't tell if her hands were tingling with the remnants of having her palms resting on Jacob's chest, or if they were now finally warming up. Soon they were not merely tingling; painful pins and needles shot from her fingertips right up her arms, and her whole hands throbbed with a deep, continuous ache.

"My hands hurt," she finally said to Jacob's back as he bent down to retrieve something from a cupboard under the sink, trying in vain to keep the plaintive note out of her voice.

"That's good," he replied as he turned and walked toward her, holding a large metal bowl. "It means they're warming up. Keep them tucked between your legs; that will help them come back to body temp slowly." Okay, she figured he knew what he was talking about, so she followed his instructions. She'd experienced cold climates before, but never been in such extreme conditions. It was easily minus twenty Celsius out there now, and only getting colder. Temperatures often dipped below freezing in her hometown of Seattle, but most of the time she was only out in the dead of winter for short bursts; going from her car to the shops, or walking down the street to the building that housed her workplace. She wasn't much of a skier, actively shunning cold winter sports for the balmy southern climes if she were to take one of her infrequent holidays. Even during her career as a marine scientist, most of her work had taken place in the warmer areas, such as the islands in the South Pacific.

"But I still can't feel my fee—" She never got to finish her sentence, as Jacob placed the bowl of water on the floor next to her and gently maneuvered both her bare feet into it.

"This is tepid water; it will help to bring the temperature of your feet up slowly." He glanced up into her face, and she suddenly saw the worry there.

"Do you think I might have frostbite?" The idea of losing a toe or two didn't appeal, and she peered down at her feet. They were red and swollen. Her stomach did a slow somersault as panic set in.

"No." His firm tone made her look up, his face level with hers as he kneeled on the floor next to her. "You don't. This is just a precaution." He sounded so sure that a surge of relief filled her. Belatedly, she wondered about his fingers and toes.

"What about you? How come you don't have your feet in water too?"

"I grew up here, I'm used to these temperatures." He stood, his scrutiny finally leaving her face. She had to extend her neck and tilt her head way back to look up at him. Gosh, he was tall. "And my police-issue gear is much superior to yours." He seemed to hesitate for a second before he added, "I'm sorry I made you hike for so long without checking your equipment was up to the task. It was remiss of me." His stilted apology caught her by surprise. Something like remorse flashed in his eyes. Did he think her nearly getting frostbite was his fault? Well, it wasn't. He was merely doing his job. If her boots were below standard, it was her own fault; she hadn't been prepared for the weather up here.

She shrugged, and said, "I guess we were in a hurry." It was true. But she had thought—naively—her clothing would withstand the temperatures. It seemed the cold in Seattle was nothing like the cold in northern Sweden.

"Yes, we were," he replied. Then, changing the subject, he said, "I'll fix us something to eat. I have soup in the freezer that will warm you up. I just need to heat it."

Nikki's stomach rumbled at the mention of soup. She'd skipped lunch in favor of the sauna and had been planning an early dinner instead. With everything that'd happened over the past few hours, she was surprised she could even think about food. But now that the adrenaline had worn off, her body was telling her she needed to eat.

"That sounds great," she replied, watching as he moved around the small hut in the capable manner she was quickly becoming accustomed to. There was an economy of movement where Jacob was concerned. Nothing seemed to fluster him, and he flowed from the freezer tucked into the corner, to the kitchen countertop and then to the microwave with a grace that surprised Nikki. Like a cat, fluid and neat, but also with an air of lethal danger about to be unleashed. She guessed that because he was a cop, a certain amount of his reserve came from his police training. But there was more than just military training at play here; there was also an air of self-confidence. A feeling that he knew who he was, and what he was capable of. He was happy in his own skin. His English was also excellent, she thought she detected a faint trace of an American twang, and she wondered briefly where he'd learned to speak it.

Her hands twinged sharply with pain, and she shuffled them around, trying to find a more comfortable position between her thighs. They were warming up now, and feeling was indeed returning to her fingers, but she almost wished for the sweet release of the numbness now that they throbbed continuously with an aching heat.

To distract herself from her hands, she asked the other question that'd been burning a hole in the fabric of her mind. "Aren't you worried that whoever is after me will turn up here?"

He turned from his task of retrieving two bowls from an overhead cupboard and fixed her with his keen gaze. Almost as if he were studying her, trying to determine whether to tell her the truth, and wondering what her reaction might be if he did. Finally, he said, "Yes, I am. But I'll know if anyone gets close to the hut. I have some…protocols in place that will sound a warning."

"You mean you have the place booby-trapped?" She swiveled her head to stare out the window, but it was pitch black out there now, and all she could see was her own reflection in the glass. Her imagination took flight as she thought about trip wires that released a deadly dart when triggered, and snares with jagged teeth ready to catch the unwary.

He gave a sudden laugh. "You Americans, I always forget how direct you can be. It's a series of laser beams and cameras, that's all," he added when he noticed the look on her face. "They're not intended to kill anyone."

"Oh, right." Of course, what had she been thinking? Her face heated, and she spun her head around to hide her embarrassment, turning her focus on taking a better look at the rest of the cabin while Jacob got on with preparing the food.

She'd noted as they'd approached his hut earlier that, unlike her holiday cabin, which was red, this one was constructed of thick, natural logs on the outside, with a small porch protecting the main door as they entered. Inside, it was just one large, open-plan room, the walls finished in more natural pine planks that looked as if they might have been hand hewn. The furs on the floor were possibly reindeer hides, giving the place even more of a rustic vibe. The wood-burning stove took up a central position, with a comfy set of couches on the opposite end from where she sat at the table next to the kitchen. Homey and practical, it was clearly old, but well cared for. Jacob had mentioned this was his family's land, and so his father had perhaps built this hut, or even his father's father before that. Nikki had heard these traditional winter huts were incredibly hard to buy and rarely, if ever, came onto the market, as they were handed down from generation to generation within a family. But where did everyone sleep? Not on the couches or the floor, surely? Then her gaze landed on a set of steep steps nestled in one corner, and she understood the bedroom, or bedrooms, must be on a second floor upstairs.

Jacob interrupted her musings when he appeared at her elbow, and said, "The food is ready. Let me help you get comfortable." He bent down and took her feet out of the bowl, wrapping them quickly in a soft, dry towel. She nearly flinched away from him, unused to having someone—especially a stranger—handle her feet. But he was gentle and professional, and she decided she quite liked his touch. And was also enjoying the view of his broad shoulders and strong neck bent below her as he tended her feet. "How are they?" he asked without looking up.

"The feeling is coming back. They're a little sore," she admitted, already knowing that was a good thing without him having to tell her. "I'm not sure I could walk too far on them right now, but I think they'll be better by tomorrow."

"Hmm." Nikki didn't like his noncommittal grunt, but before she could make further comments, he placed a bowl of steaming soup on the table next to her, and the smell made Nikki's mouth water like crazy. She swiveled in her seat so she was facing the food, careful to keep her feet bundled up in the towel.

"Oh, wow." She wafted her nose down over the bowl. "What is it? Beef and vegetable?"

"Close. It's moose and vegetable," he corrected.

She'd never tasted moose before. But then her stomach rumbled, and she decided she was game for just about anything right now. "Did you make this?" she asked, leaning over to take another sniff. It smelled delicious, so she picked up her spoon. But her fingers were painful and slightly swollen, and she found she couldn't hold the utensil properly.

"Are you okay? I can help if you like?" He leaned toward her, as if ready to grab her spoon, concern etched on his face.

"No, no, I can do it," she assured him. She might look awkward, holding the spoon in her fist rather than between her fingers, but it was infinitely less awkward than having him spoon-feed her like a baby.

He sat down and picked up his own spoon. "Yes, I made this," he confirmed. "I haven't hunted recently, so this has been in the freezer since late summer, but it should still be good."

Nikki's spoon stalled halfway to her mouth. "You mean you killed the moose?" She was eating an animal that Jacob had shot? Why did the idea shock her? Hunting was a big sport in America; her cousins, who lived in Montana, were avid huntsmen, even though she'd politely refused to take part whenever they invited her on one of her rare visits. And part of her knew that hunting was a big part of the Swedish culture as well. But still… It changed her concept of Jacob ever so slightly. Not necessarily for the worse, but more that it cemented in her head he could be a dangerous man if the need arose.

"Of course," he replied matter-of-factly. "The moose was on my land—my family's land—and we never take too many, just what we need."

"Yes, yes," she nodded her head in agreement, putting the stalled spoon to her lips. "Oh, this is freaking delicious." It was good, hot and with a satisfying dash of spicy pepper. "I've never tasted moose before, but I think I'm a convert," she said through another mouthful of food. The heat of the soup warmed her from the inside, and she finally began to feel almost normal again.

He gave a shy smile at her compliment, the dimple reappearing, and against her better judgement, she decided she was beginning to like Jacob. Not only was he strong, with a tough exterior, but it seemed he had a softer side; a man who could cook this well was a rare find indeed.

They ate in silence for a few moments, Nikki savoring the gamey taste of the meat, mixed with carrots and celery and what might be barley. It was a good, hearty soup, exactly what she needed. It didn't escape her how unreal this whole scenario was. Eating soup with a police officer who'd just rescued her from a deadly threat, and they were now holed up in his isolated winter hut in the middle of a Swedish forest. Never in her wildest dreams could she have conjured up this scenario. If only Tammy could've known when she suggested this holiday, she might've…

Nikki stopped eating, remembering that her colleague was dead. It seemed unbelievable. Beautiful, bubbly Tammy. A US Fulbright Fellow, a staunch advocate for the preservation of the Nordic fjord ecosystems, passionate about her job at the institute, a brilliant teacher and a loyal friend. Tammy was twenty years older than Nikki but had taken her under her wing when she first joined the institute seven years ago, and they'd formed a strong bond ever since.

And Antoine, earnest and accomplished, but also with that very French dry sense of humor when the mood took him. He was one of the young interns who joined the institute every year to bring their energy and knowledge for their chosen environmental causes to the forefront. She wasn't as familiar with Antoine, having only met him a few weeks before this planned trip to Norway, but she liked and respected him. Why would anyone want her friends dead? They'd done nothing to harm anyone, had no enemies that Nikki could fathom.

She placed her spoon on the table, her appetite suddenly replaced with a heavy stone of grief in the pit of her stomach. So many questions tumbled through her head.

Jacob sensed her change in mood and also stopped eating, a question in the lift of his eyebrow.

But before Nikki could put one of the many issues into words, a satellite phone on a small side table jangled with an incoming call. Jacob sat up straighter, fixing the phone with his sharp gaze. Then he stood quickly, grabbing it, answering it after only the second ring.

"Hello." He sounded just as officious as he had when he'd first burst into her sauna, speaking with a stilted bluntness, and she understood he must be speaking to a superior, but at least still in English so she could understand. "Yes, Deputy Commissioner, I have her here with me." Nikki watched Jacob's features intently, trying to read any subtle changes that'd let her know what else was being said. But he was very good at keeping his thoughts carefully hidden, his answers monosyllabic. A gust of frustrated air left her lips, and she sat back in her chair and folded her arms, staring daggers at him. She wasn't sure about ranks in the Swedish police, but if it were anything like the American cops, then a deputy commissioner must be fairly high up. Which meant she was important. But why?

Soon, it became too much for her to bear; she needed to hear what was going on. They were speaking about her. And about her friends. She had a right to know. She leaned forward so that she was directly in Jacob's line of sight and caught his eye, wrinkling her brow and pressing her lips together in a silent plea to be let in on the conversation.

He shook his head and turned slightly away.

Oh no, he wasn't getting away with it that easily.

She went to stand, and sharp pains shot through her feet, sending her quickly back to her seat. Shit, they were much sorer than she thought. She tried again, this time easing her weight up slowly, leaning on the table for support. She found she could stand, but her feet felt like they were on fire. At least she now had Jacob's attention; he'd moved around the table, concern etched into the lines on his forehead, the phone still clamped tightly to one ear. If she could not walk, she could still make her point, so she tilted her chin up and put her hands on hips, daring him to ignore her now.

He watched her for a few seconds, still listening intently to whatever the deputy commissioner was saying, and she thought he was going to continue to disregard her silent appeal, until he surprised her by suddenly saying, "Can I put you on speaker, sir? Nik…Dr. Winter would like to hear what we're saying."

There was a moment of silence while Nikki waited impatiently, and then Jacob laid the phone on the table in front of them both. "This is Biträdande Poliskommissarie Runar Staaf, the deputy commissioner of the northern regional head of police," he said by way of introduction, nodding at Nikki to speak. Gratefully, she sat down and gathered her thoughts.

"Hello, Deputy Commissioner Staaf. Can I ask how my…" she nearly choked on the words and had to clear her throat. "How my colleagues died?" The room went misty as her eyes filled with sudden tears, but she fought them back. Now wasn't the time. She'd have time to grieve for her lost friends later. Now, she was going to do everything in her power to make sure whoever did this was caught and thrown in jail for life. At least the shock of the news of their deaths was wearing off. Jacob's blunt statement back in the holiday hut had been so horrifying that her body had reacted the only way it could; by blocking out the terrible revelation. But now, the anguish was quickly being replaced with anger, a burning need for redemption for her coworkers. In some ways, maybe she could thank Jacob for his brutal revealing of the truth; perhaps it was a little like ripping off a Bandaid. Short and sharp, but necessary.

The last time she'd seen Tammy and Antoine, they'd been about to join a scientific vessel conducting research in the Norwegian fjords; their version of a holiday was to keep doing what they loved. One of the lead scientists was a colleague of Tammy's from the University of Oregon, where she lectured, and he had asked her and Antoine to come with him. There was a spot on the boat for Nikki too, but she'd turned it down, feeling the need to spend some quality time alone on a proper holiday, somewhere away from phones and computers and all technology. Which was when Tammy had suggested the hut owned by a friend of a friend, Andreas.

Briefly, Nikki wondered *what if*. What if she'd gone on the trip with them? Would she be dead now too?

There was a brief pause on the other end of the phone before the deputy commissioner replied gruffly, "Hello, Dr. Winter, I'm sorry for your loss." The man's English was good, but his accent was much heavier than Jacob's, and Nikki had to concentrate to make out his words. "And I'm equally sorry you're in such a predicament. In most normal cases, I would not have agreed to bring you into this conversation. But this case is very different. At least you will understand what kind of people we're dealing with if I tell you everything we know." The deputy commissioner took another momentary pause, as if gathering his thoughts. "The man, Antoine Claudet, drowned while scuba diving on a science research boat near Skarberget in Tysfjord fjord with a team of six divers."

Nikki covered her mouth to stifle a gasp as her eyes once again filled with unwanted tears. Jacob reached down and briefly touched her shoulder, his message of condolence clear. When Tammy had suggested it, Antoine had jumped at the chance to go scuba diving in the Norwegian fjords in winter. He'd been so excited to dive there, going on and on about how crystal clear the water would be, talking about how he might even come face to face with a wild orca. It was always more challenging to complete a cold-water dive, but the experience made it all worthwhile, he'd said with glee. The thought of all that freezing water, even wearing the thickest of dry suits, made Nikki quake in her boots.

The deputy commissioner continued, "It was a night dive, which they tell me is common for this site, but it seems he didn't resurface with the rest of the group."

"Oh, no," Nikki whispered. What could've possibly gone wrong? Antoine was always prattling about how much care needed to be taken on these night dives. Everyone had a buddy, and they always stayed within sight of each other.

"They couldn't mount a proper search until first light the next morning," the deputy commissioner went on. "They found his body caught in a tall stand of kelp forest halfway down the cliff wall. His scuba tank had run out of air."

Even though Antoine was pedantic about things like checking his oxygen levels and staying within sight of a scuba buddy, it still sounded like a tragic accident to Nikki. Why did they think this might've been murder?

"So, what about Tammy?" she asked, even though her stomach roiled at the thought of hearing the answer.

"Yes, well, as you know, Tammy was on the same boat as Antoine, and the entire team returned to Bodø after the tragedy so she could begin making arrangements for his body to be shipped back to France. Of course, even though they still all thought this was a terrible accident, an autopsy was required, and so the family would have to wait until that was completed."

God, that must've been so horrific for Tammy. Dealing with Antoine's death, talking to his family, relaying the sad news to the institute, negotiating a strange country's laws regarding death and funerals and waiting for the autopsy results so they could release the body. For a second, Nikki wondered why Tammy hadn't contacted her, but the answer was obvious. She'd probably tried, but Nikki had been so intent on staying off the grid, remaining blissfully ignorant and technology free, she hadn't once turned on the satellite phone Andreas had left with her as a safety precaution. Nikki thumped the palm of her hand onto her forehead. Stupid. Stupid. How could she have been so selfish? Jacob's warm hand landed on her shoulder once more, and she drew strength from his compassion, still not really wanting to hear what came next.

"Reports stated Tammy fell to her death from the eighth-story balcony of her Bodø hotel. This was three days after the death of Antoine, and at first everyone thought it was an awful coincidence."

Yes, she could understand why, because it did look like a terrible, horrible, unimaginable twist of fate. But she was getting an inkling of what might be going on here. The only thing that made sense. The only thing that might link the two murders. The idea was almost too preposterous to even consider. Surely no one would stoop to that level? Surely, people weren't so inflamed by greed that they would take another person's life?

"A fall from a balcony is not that uncommon. People fall more than you would expect. They lean too far over the railing so they can see something, or they sit on the railing because they're too confident of their own abilities. Or they are just drunk and do things most sober people would not contemplate. You'd be surprised at how often it happens. There were also suspicions that perhaps it was a suicide; sometimes, the death of a close friend can affect people like that. So, as you can imagine, we had many things to contemplate, and murder was not really on our radar."

No, she would never do that; she would never take her own life, Nikki wanted to retort, but the deputy commissioner was already speaking again. "After the media reported her death, however, a witness came forward and said they thought they had seen someone on the balcony with Tammy right before she fell."

Nikki grasped. "So she was pushed."

"Maybe. Witnesses are not always reliable; they can get room numbers wrong, floor levels wrong, or you get people who want their fifteen minutes of fame and fabricate stories just to get themselves on the news. But Tammy was supposed to be alone in her room, and the hotel reported that none of the staff had accessed her room; they can tell by the records of the individual swipe cards of each staff member. Tammy hadn't ordered any room service or reported any issue that would require a staff member to go into her room, so it made us wonder."

"But who had access to her room? If someone pushed her, how did they get in?"

"We don't know yet. It could be as simple as they knocked on the door and she let them in. She wouldn't have had any reason to suspect someone wanted to do her harm," the deputy commissioner replied.

Nikki glanced across at Jacob, who was listening avidly to everything the deputy commissioner said. It seemed as if he was hearing this for the first time too. He raised an inquiring eyebrow in her direction, but said nothing, waiting for the deputy commissioner to go on.

"It wasn't until I talked to the president of your Marine Conservation Institute, Dr. Morgan, that we thought perhaps something more sinister might be going on. He told me that the three of you were all working on the same project, investigating the Nordic fish farms belonging to Diàoyú Aquaculture, and that's when alarm bells began to ring. So we went back and took a closer look into Antoine's death." The deputy commissioner paused to draw breath, but the hair on the back of Nikki's neck was already standing on end; she didn't like where this was going.

"By that time his scuba gear had all been sent away to be tested, which is common practice when someone passes away while diving. It was found that his tank pressure gauge wasn't reading properly, and we now think he had less than half a tank of air when he went down instead of a full tank as his pressure gauge indicated. It seems his diving gear may have been tampered with. We don't know how he got tangled in the kelp; maybe he panicked when he realized he was running out of air. The autopsy results also came back to show that the cause of death was drowning, which corresponds with our findings." She could almost hear the deputy commissioner shrug on the other end of the phone, but she couldn't be so blasé about the way Antoine had died. He must've been so scared, panicking, alone and afraid down in the dark depths. It made her feel sick just to think about it.

Of course, the deputy commissioner couldn't know what she was thinking, and he continued on with his explanation. "We also questioned his dive buddy about why he absconded from Antoine's side, and he told us he had to surface early when he found he had an equipment issue."

"Leaving Antoine alone to fend for himself," Nikki replied quietly.

"Yes. And once we knew what to look for, it seemed his dive buddy's equipment failure may have also been sabotage, this time a defective depth gauge. At first we considered it might've been someone on the boat who damaged the gear, which would have narrowed our suspect list down significantly. But the boat was docked overnight, and everyone slept ashore, so the equipment could have been tampered with during the day before they left for the dive. Once we discovered all of this, Dr. Morgan insisted we contact you as he thought there might also be a threat to your life. And I agreed with him."

Russell Morgan's face swam into focus in her mind. Such a kind man, and it showed in his features; he was always smiling, always encouraging his staff, reminding her of a benevolent uncle. Deep brown eyes, full of empathy, and a swathe of long, gray hair he kept tied up in a man bun. He often admitted to being a bit of a hippy at heart, although he was as smart as they came; his intelligence and dedication to the marine center were some of the major factors that kept driving it to excellence.

The deputy commissioner spoke again, and Nikki dragged her thoughts back to the present. "Dr. Morgan also mentioned that Dr. Tammy Pittman was due to present your findings at a court case in two weeks' time. So now we believe we have a motive."

"Those bastards," Nikki whispered as her worst fears were realized.

"Whatever you found out there on your research expedition is causing a problem. A very big problem," the deputy commissioner said, oblivious to Nikki's pain. "Might be highly damaging for the company involved. It seems like someone is trying to prevent the court from hearing the information you gathered by killing the people who did the testing and trying to make all their research disappear. We now know both Tammy and Antoine's work computers are missing." The deputy commissioner's tone was ominous now.

The idea was so farcical that she could hardly wrap her head around it. Yes, Tammy had been slated to give evidence in a court case, and yes, their recent findings would indeed be damning for Diàoyú Aquaculture. Hopefully enough to shut the company down for good, but at the very least stop them using their corrupt fish farming techniques in the fjords. But was this really a case of corporate greed? She'd heard the term used many times before. Power brokers with a shocking agenda who thought they were above the law. But surely no company took themselves that seriously? How could anyone decide to choose profits over human life? Tammy and Antoine had been good people, making a difference in the world, and someone had brushed them aside as if they were less important than pawns on a chessboard. For what? To make more money?

"You must be joking," Nikki whispered softly, still unable to believe it could be true.

"I'm sorry to say I'm dead serious," the deputy commissioner replied. "It looks like this company is determined to make sure your team's findings never see the light of day. According to Dr. Morgan, it could mean millions —perhaps even billions of dollars—in lost revenue for the company if Tammy, or any of your team, were to testify in front of the Norwegian court. We believe that this company— or someone in this company—now has you squarely in its sights."

"Yes, but…" Nikki covered her mouth, but not before a small groan of fear left her lips. This couldn't be happening. How could a simple data collection expedition turn into this deadly game of assassination? Both she and Tammy had been called to give evidence at court cases as expert witnesses many times before, but she could never have dreamed that she could be targeted for telling the truth. It was beyond imagination. The kind of thing that happened in Matt Damon movies, not in real life.

Two thoughts echoed around in her head. Tammy and Antoine were dead. And she was going to be next. Everything suddenly became so real that her panic turned to pure dread, making her hands shake uncontrollably. Bile rose in her throat, and she knew she was going to be sick. She clamped her hand more tightly over her mouth, but it did no good; her stomach heaved, then emptied itself, and she leaned over and vomited all over the wooden floor.

CHAPTER FOUR

"Oh, gosh, I'm so sorry." Nikki looked stricken as she stared down at the mess she'd made on the floor.

But Jacob was more worried about the woman than about the vomit. He'd ended the call with the deputy commissioner, saying he'd call him back soon, then stood behind her, rubbing small circles on her back, watching her thin shoulders shudder until her violent retching had finally ended. Now as he stood over her, a strange impulse to take her into his arms, to protect her from what was to come, nearly overwhelmed him. He hunkered down beside her, careful not to kneel in the muck. Her face was so pale, her eyes so big and wide, it made her seem childlike and vulnerable.

"Don't worry about it," he said, fighting back the urge to gaze deep into her eyes and tell her everything would be alright, that he vowed to keep her safe. God, he wanted her to be safe. But he'd always been a man who kept his promises, no matter what. And after his failure to protect Tristan, this wasn't a promise he was sure he could keep.

"I'll clean it up," she said, and made as if to stand, but he kept a steady pressure on her shoulder.

"I'll do it. You need to stay off your feet." He busied

himself finding a bucket, a cloth, and some rubber gloves in the small laundry off the mudroom. The horrific details of how and why her friends had died, added to the threat now placed on her life, had been too much for her. He wanted to kick himself for letting her join in the conversation. As a cop, he'd become desensitized to this sort of thing, and he should've remembered that. At least she hadn't fainted this time. But in some ways, this had been worse. The look of pure terror in her eyes was like a spear through his gut. It would've been better if he'd talked to the deputy commissioner alone. That way he could decide what to tell her and when, keeping it on a need to know basis. Now she knew everything, and the idea terrified her. And him.

When he came back into the room, he found her standing, a grimace of pain on her pretty face as she took a step away from the table.

"Where are you going? Sit down," he commanded.

"But..." she gestured to the recently digested soup now spread all over his floor.

"No buts, I said I'd clean it up."

She gave him a murderous stare and continued to stand, holding out her hand for the cloth and bucket. Stubborn woman. At least the desperate fear was gone now; that was a small mercy. A woman's tears had always been his kryptonite.

He ignored the daggers she was shooting in his direction and filled the bucket at the sink, pulled on the gloves, then got down on his hands and knees to wipe the floor clean. A small growl of frustration erupted from behind him, and he had to hide a smile. She might be stubborn, but his mother had always said that he was as headstrong as they came; she was no match for him.

As a way to distract her, as well as try to get his head around the facts of this case, he asked, "What do fish farms have to do with court cases and people wanting to commit murder?" Without taking his gaze away from his task, he noted in his periphery that she sat back in the chair.

For a moment, he thought she might not answer, but eventually, she said, "It's kind of a long story." At least her voice sounded stronger now, not helpless, as it had before. Good, at least she was thinking straight again. Using that scientific brain and not allowing herself to descend into chaos. "Do you know much about where the salmon in all the supermarkets comes from?" she asked.

He lifted onto his knees to wash the cloth in the bucket and shook his head.

"Ocean-based fish farms produce roughly seventy percent of the world's salmon. And Norway supplies over half of that farmed fish."

Jacob gave a surprised whistle. It wasn't something he often thought about. He rarely ate the tasty, pink-fleshed fish, but when he did, it was usually with his family. And they used their Sámi traditional methods to catch them in the early summer from the rivers as they came to spawn. He was one of the lucky few who were spoiled with the luxury of eating wild-caught salmon.

"Yes, it's a multi-billion dollar industry," she replied. "But the Norwegian government has always allocated farm licenses sparingly; they understand the need to protect the pristine waters of their fjords. Which is a great thing for the environment. However, even with all their protocols in place, the aquaculture operations, especially those in the fjords, are putting huge stresses on the waterways," Nikki emphasized the words by tapping the tabletop, and Jacob stopped what he was doing to raise his gaze. Her face had become animated, her big, blue eyes, which had been full of despair, were now sparkling, her forehead puckered as she leaned forward, intent on her conversation. "So, Norway has been looking for ways to make a change. For starters, the Chinese and Norwegian governments have collaborated to build the world's biggest mobile fish farm. A huge floating monstrosity that gives me the creeps." She shuddered theatrically, and he smiled at her touch of melodrama. "But it has revolutionized the way they farm fish in the ocean." She lifted her shoulders as if to say the big boat may be better than the farms, but she still didn't have to agree with it. "In the past few years there's also been a movement toward creating land-based fish farms, which will ease the pressure on the oceans considerably."

"That all sounds positive. So what does all this have to do with you?" he questioned, wondering how she and her team had been dragged into a court case if everything was slowly winding down to be converted to terrestrial farming.

"As you can imagine, a lot of the old aquaculture practices are now becoming obsolete, and Norway is looking to reduce the number of leases and start shutting down the farms—apart from the more sustainable large-boat ones, that is. Needless to say, some of the companies are very unhappy about this and are refusing to go. Some of the smaller businesses and individuals were already winding down anyway, as they struggled to compete with the bigger corporations, who've signed huge contracts to export fish to Japan or America. But a lot of the larger ones are resisting. One Chinese company in particular, Diàoyú Aquaculture, is turning out to be a thorn in the side of the Norwegian government, using delaying tactics such as pleading their case to the courts and tying everything up with red tape. It also seems there's a bit of dissent within Norwegian ruling lines as well. Some of the left-wing politicians want the farms to stay and are—unbelievably—on the side of the Chinese company. I personally think there's a lot of corruption going on. Who knows, maybe the Norwegian administration is even getting some political pressure from the Chinese administration. Or a more likely scenario is that one or more of the leading political figures are receiving under the table payments to keep the fish farms right where they are." She pouted, pursing her pretty lips into a bow. "Anyway," she continued, shaking her head as if to rid it of wayward thoughts. "One way to force them out is to prove they aren't complying with the strict environmental regulations."

A light bulb went on in Jacob's head. "And that's where you come in?"

"Yes," she said with a delighted smile. "Russell… Dr. Morgan, was asked to put together a team to document levels of plastic pollution from Diàoyú farms by the Norwegian minister for fisheries and oceans. To become a world leader in aquaculture, Norway has relied on its rigorous guidelines, close monitoring and sustained commitment to development. And now they can hopefully use the same guidelines to help them shut down this Chinese company. One of the biggest problems with ocean-based fish farms is the amount of plastic pollution they produce. I've been documenting the types and quantities of plastic these farms release into the ocean over the past seven years, and the stats would blow your mind."

"I'm sure they would."

"If the Norwegian government can prove Diàoyú is breaking the regulations set up to guard against plastic contamination around the farms, then they can get rid of the company once and for all."

"And you and your team have that proof?" Jacob said slowly.

"Yes, we do. Or we did," she added, faltering slightly. "The data still needs to be collated, but there was obvious evidence that Diàoyú hadn't put any of the procedures in place to stop plastic waste from entering the waterways. They were flouting the law and didn't give a shit—pardon my French—about anything but making more money. It's a lot cheaper if they just let all the plastics float away, clogging up the aquatic environments and killing the marine life, rather than set up complicated methods to control and dispose of it."

"I see." Jacob got to his feet, taking the bucket with him, the floor now clean and vomit-free. "Give me a second," he said, and took everything to the laundry where he cleaned up and pulled off the gloves. "Go on." He returned to the kitchen area, leaning one hip lightly against the tabletop as he listened to her speak.

"It's not just the plastic debris you see washed up on the beaches that's the problem, although it makes up a large part of our data collection. It's the microplastics that are often more cause for worry. And the issue is, it's sometimes so hard to quantify. We still don't really understand the long-lasting effects of microplastics on the planet." She rested her chin in her palm and stared out the window, unseeing, her mind caught up in figuring out this environmental riddle. Her long, blonde hair fell down over her shoulders, all those silken tresses mesmerizing him for a moment, so that he almost forgot what he wanted to say, giving her time to continue talking. "The rapid rise of the aquaculture industry is scaring quite a few people. Right now it's touted as one of the world's most sustainable ways to produce protein for human consumption. But plastic pollution from fish farming is often underquantified. If left unmanaged, we're afraid it will have huge detrimental effects on both marine environments and people's health."

She continued to stare out at the dark forest. "Tammy and Antoine believed implicitly in what we were doing. We all wanted to save the ocean environment from annihilation by greedy companies who only want one thing. Money. They were both so passionate about this cause. They were trying to rescue us from ourselves. And now they've paid the ultimate price for their altruism. Why?" She turned to look at him, her mouth downturned, a single tear trickling down her cheek. Her hands were clenched into fists on the tabletop. "Why did they have to die? What's the point of it all? Why are human beings so intent on destroying everything they touch?" Another tear fell, and Jacob moved to stand closer to her chair. "Why?" It was merely a whisper now, almost like a plea for salvation. *Fann*, here came the tears.

"I don't know," he answered. He'd seen the absolute worst of humanity in his role over the past ten years. He knew people killed for all sorts of reasons, avarice and greed often big motivators. At times, he'd become jaded and embittered by society; it was Mårten who usually buoyed him out of his dismal moods. Mårten always found a silver lining; he was the optimist of their partnership. Without Mårten's positive attitude, it was up to him to help her out of this dark place.

"But it's people like you who make this world a better place." Gently, he covered one of her hands with his, careful of her sore fingers, and she looked up into his face. She wore her pain and compassion in the downturn of her lips and the scrunch of her forehead. Even with red-rimmed eyes and tears leaking down her cheeks, she was one of the most beautiful women he'd ever seen.

Without thinking, he leaned in and used the thumb of his other hand to wipe the teardrop from her cheek. She stilled beneath his touch, her eyes widening. Up close, he could see a darker smudge of indigo outlining the baby blue of her irises. His gaze traveled down her face, landing on her mouth. What would her lips taste like?

Oh, *faan*, he wanted to kiss her. The realization hit him like a punch.

He tried to conjure up images of Freya, hoping to distract himself. His current lover was bright and intelligent, with a considerable aptitude for sex. But instead of distracting him, thinking of Freya only heightened his need for Nikki. He hated to admit it, but Freya's lips came in a poor second to Nikki's luscious, plump ones. He leaned in just a little closer.

This wasn't good. Not good at all. He was letting his libido get in the way again. If he kissed her, it'd jeopardize this mission, jeopardize her safety. But, oh, she was so…tempting.

A buzzing sound cut through his conscience, but he was so ensnared by her mouth that he ignored it at first. It wasn't until she broke their gaze and turned her head toward the noise that it dawned on him. It was coming from one of the alarms he'd set up as a warning if anyone approached the hut.

Shit. Someone was coming.

He had to get her out of here to safety, no matter what the cost.

"We've got to go," he said, tugging her to her feet. "Right now."

He couldn't fail again.

CHAPTER FIVE

Jacob stood tense and silent beside her, head tilted to the side, listening keenly to the low buzzing noise that'd broken their connection. He'd been staring straight into her eyes. So close. Touching her face. Had he been about to kiss her? Had she even wanted him to kiss her? Damn that noise. Now she might never know.

"What's happening?" Nikki half-whispered, unsure about the need to stay quiet as he continued to stand rigid and unmoving beside her. Her voice seemed to galvanize him into action, but instead of an answer, Jacob swept her up into his arms and carried her back toward the mudroom, flicking off the light switch as he went, plunging everything into darkness. Only the glow of the fire remained, and soon even that was gone as he let the door swing shut behind them. He felt his way along the wall and then lowered her gently onto the bench seat.

"What the…?" Jacob's finger landed on her lips.

"We need to stay quiet," he whispered. This was all getting a little strange, but she'd go with it. For now. He pulled out his phone, and she watched his face light up with the ghostly digital glow. "*Fann.*" He'd used this word before, and while Nikki didn't know what it meant, she could guess the underlying sentiment.

He put his phone back in his pocket, and she listened to him groping around in the near darkness, then he thrust something into her lap. "Put this on." Careful of her sore fingers, she explored the pile of fabric, deciding it was some sort of winter clothing, maybe a snowsuit like the one Jacob had been wearing earlier, along with some fur-lined boots. She remembered he'd mentioned he had a spare commando suit when they'd first arrived at his hut. A small amount of firelight filtered through a window high in the door to the mudroom. It wasn't much, but her eyes were adjusting quickly so that she could hold the suit out in front of her and work out which way was up. The small window silhouetted Jacob as he bobbed up and down, huffing a little with the effort, and she understood he was also getting dressed.

Which meant only one thing. They were going back outside into the freezing temperatures. In the dark. And then it dawned on her. That buzzing sound had been an alarm. One of Jacob's laser beams, or cameras, or whatever he had out there, must've triggered, and this was a warning that someone had approached. Coming for her. The thought made her go as still as a statue, fear pervading every cell. Tears pricked at her eyelids. She'd thought she could relax once they'd made it to Jacob's hut. Stupid really, because of course the danger had followed her here. She wanted all of this just to go away. Wished with all her heart she could continue to stay safe and warm in Jacob's little hut, enjoying a bowl of soup with a good-looking man and not have to worry about a murderous psychopath coming to kill her.

There was a sudden presence hovering in front of her, Jacob's face very close to hers. A white knit hat covered his dark hair, but she caught a glint as his eyes reflected the light seeping through the window. "Are you okay?" he asked, concern edging the urgency in his voice. Her fear coalesced into a cold, hard lump in the pit of her stomach, but his presence removed the numbing paralysis from her limbs. This man would keep her safe. He would make sure she made it out of here alive. She'd trusted him so far, she just had to keep on trusting him. His skills and training would get them through.

Drawing in a deep breath, she nodded, then realized he probably couldn't see. "Yes. Yes, sorry," she replied in a hurry.

"Good. I have a snowmobile parked in the shed next to the hut. We're going to use it to get out of here. You'll need to follow my lead. Now quickly, get dressed." He stood and went over to the door that led outside, peering through another small window.

"Is someone coming?" She had to ask the question. Had to know for sure what was going on.

"Yes," he answered simply. "Two people as far as I can tell." At least he wasn't pulling any punches. She wanted to ask more, like how close they were, and had they spotted the hut yet, but kept her mouth shut.

Stirred into action, she wriggled her legs into the suit and then proceeded to stand so she could pull it on and nearly toppled back onto the bench as pain seared through her. She'd forgotten about her feet. They were still sore and swollen. But she had no choice; Jacob was already dressed and waiting. She was holding him up, wasting precious time while possible hired hitmen neared the hut. They might even be outside right now, sizing up the place, getting ready to storm through the door. The image spurred her on, and she gritted her teeth as she got slowly to her feet, levering herself off the seat until most of her weight was in her legs. This time it was bearable, but she swayed a little as she struggled to get both arms into the suit and then do up the zip, using the wall to help her balance. Lifting one foot, she delicately wedged it into the boot opening. She wasn't wearing any socks, but there was no time to ask about that now. The boots were too big, but that was probably a godsend. If they'd been too tight, she would never have got her damaged feet into them. Once she'd forced her feet past the pain and had them on, she found it was easier to stand; she could put all her weight on her feet now and the fur lining was soft against her tender skin.

"I'm ready," she announced quietly, drawing in a deep breath, clenching her fists on her thighs. She felt a bit like the abominable snowman in this suit, three sizes too large for her. It would hinder her movement, but she braced herself anyway, ready to go on his command.

"Good." He turned away from his scrutiny of the window. "Put this on. It will be freezing on the snowmobile." Without asking, he tugged a white balaclava down over her head, his gloved fingers brushing the side of her face, reminding her for a second how he'd touched her cheek so tenderly only a few moments before. Then, he also pushed a knit beanie over the top of her head. Perhaps a little overkill, but after her experience today in this fierce cold, maybe he was right to overdress her. His hands left her, and this time she really did feel like the abominable snowman with the balaclava leaving only her eyes showing. "And these." He thrust a pair of gloves into her hands, but as he watched her pull them on, his head sprang up and he stared intently at the door leading back into the main room.

"Don't move," he ordered, and disappeared into the hut before she could even open her mouth. *What now?* She froze, unsure of what was happening. Five seconds later, he re-emerged through the door carrying her backpack. "Wear it on the front," he said, and so she slipped it over her shoulders so that it covered her chest. Thank the Lord he'd remembered. She broke out in a cold sweat at the thought they'd almost left it behind. All the data she'd collected over the past two weeks was stored on this computer. Now more than ever, it became critical that she not lose her research. Tammy and Antoine had died because of what they knew, their computers and all their records missing. She would not let these bastards win that easily. It was then that she noticed Jacob also had a white backpack slung across his chest as well, but she had no time to ask what was in it.

"Stay as close to me as you can," he instructed. "We're going out and to the right." It was only then she noted the gun was back in his hand, and a chill ran down her spine. This was real. He was armed and dangerous and expecting trouble. She nodded and stood behind him, awaiting his next move.

Slowly, he cracked the door open; the blast of razor-sharp air took her breath away. It was dark, but not as dark as she'd expected. A quarter moon hung low in the sky, and the snow glowed in the moonlight, making the shadows seem darker and every tree stand out in stark relief. Nothing moved out there. But Jacob waited. And waited. Her feet throbbed inside her boots. At last, he took a step out through the door and onto the front porch, every move predatory as she followed on his heels. They crept down the stairs, hugging the front of the hut as she followed the path he made for her through the thigh-high snowdrifts, her poor feet protesting at every step. Nikki flinched at every sound, expecting someone to come charging across the small clearing, or bullets to fly in their direction. Only the hoot of a distant owl and the gentle rush of snow falling from a branch filled the silence. Otherwise, it was eerily quiet.

Just as he'd said, a little shed hugged the side of the house, and Jacob stopped to scrutinize their surroundings one last time before pulling off his glove and keying in a code that undid a large padlock. The double doors opened inwards, leading them into a narrow but surprisingly long building. It was too dark to see much inside, so Nikki grabbed at Jacob's suit, holding on and following behind him as best as she was able.

There was a loud rustling sound, and she caught the gleam of metal as Jacob pulled a tarpaulin off, revealing a large snowmobile.

"You hop on the back," he commanded in a whisper. "Then when I climb on, hang on to me as tight as you can. This is going to happen fast; we have to get across the clearing and into the trees."

Even though her insides trembled like a bowl of jelly, she swung her leg over the wide seat and settled herself against the bar at the back, waiting. Her cousins owned a couple of snowmobiles, and so she was familiar with the machine, having driven one herself a few times over the years when she visited Montana. But that'd never been in the pitch dark, in unfamiliar countryside.

Jacob was suddenly in front of her, straddling the seat, inserting a key into the ignition. The machine coughed and died the first time he pushed the start button. "Come on, you piece of shit," he muttered. Then it roared to life, the guttural engine almost deafening within the confines of the shed. "Hold on," he called, and she scrambled to wrap her arms around his middle as he let out the throttle. Hampered slightly by the backpack she wore on her front, which was now wedged between them, she managed to grip his waist as tightly as possible. She suddenly understood why he'd told her to wear the pack frontwards, because now that it was safely sandwiched in the middle, there was less chance of her losing it. Her body, encased in Jacob's snow camouflage, also shielded the pack so it no longer stood out against the all-white surroundings.

The sled rolled forward, and they were out into the open and speeding over the blanket of snow before she knew it. A loud crack sounded off to their left, audible even over the din of the roaring engine. Two more cracks followed in quick succession, and Jacob swerved the sled sideways, zigzagging his way across the clearing.

Was that...? Another crack and something whizzed past her ear.

A bullet.

Someone was shooting at them.

Nikki turned to look back over her shoulder as a figure emerged from the treeline. He lifted a rifle and took aim. "Watch out!" she screamed, and ducked instinctively, burying her head into Jacob's back. A bullet cut the air near her as Jacob turned the snowmobile sharply to the left. She hung on for dear life while Jacob threw the machine from left to right and then left again. More bullets buzzed past and Nikki tensed, waiting for the biting pain of one embedding in her back. But it never came, and all of a sudden dark tree trunks reared up on either side as they slid beneath the first branches of the forest.

Safe. Were they safe now they were no longer out in the open?

Jacob slowed once they were under the trees, but not as much as Nikki would've liked. They were traveling through dense woodland, not following a trail, let alone a road, and he maintained what Nikki considered to be a breakneck speed. He probably knew this forest like the back of his hand, but she remained terrified and continued to cling to him like a limpet. If her fear hadn't been so great, she might've been able to enjoy the feel of his firm abs underneath the snowsuit tensing as he rode, but right now all she cared about was hanging on long enough to get away from that shooter.

Ten minutes later, he slowed, coming to a complete stop beneath the cover of a copse of birch trees. Their trunks glowed palely in the moonlight as Nikki dared to lift her head and look around. Cutting the engine, he turned to the side so he could look down at her. She hadn't noticed at the time, but he'd pulled up the loose folds of his suit's neckline to cover his mouth and nose as they left the shed, so that only his eyes were showing under the brim of his white beanie. Clumps of icy snow clung to the fabric, where his moist breath had frozen as it hit the arctic air. She must have similar icicles on her balaclava and was silently grateful for his quick thinking; otherwise, she might be sporting a frost-bitten nose right now to add to her hands and feet. An almost otherworldly silence settled over them, and she was more than glad he was here with her; she would've been completely lost out in this dark wilderness.

"Are you okay?" Jacob barked, eyes boring into her face. "You weren't hurt?"

"No. No, I'm fine. But that was real. That man really shot at us," she panted, her breath forming a silver cloud as she tugged up her balaclava.

"Yes," Jacob replied, his mouth a grim line. "But you did a great job hanging on." His gaze met hers, and his tone softened. "We've bought a little time. They were on foot, which means they'll have to go back and regroup before they can follow us."

"Are you sure?" she asked. "They could have snowmobiles too." She swiveled and half stood at the thought, expecting to hear pursuing engines cutting through the stillness.

"No, they didn't. I would've seen it on my camera if they did." His calm words reassured her, and she sat back down on the vinyl seat. "My hut can only be accessed on foot or by snowmobile. There's only one road leading into this area, so I leave my car parked about fifteen minutes away, then use the snowmobile to go the rest of the way." Her heart lifted at the idea of a vehicle. To her, it sounded like safety and warmth, a way to escape this dangerous situation and return to civilization. "But I think it's too dangerous to go back to my car right now. It's on the opposite side of the hut. We'd have to take the risk of going back past those men." His words harpooned her burgeoning hope.

"Oh, really?" She tried not to let her disappointment show. Where else were they supposed to go? The idea of being stuck out here all night wasn't in the least bit appealing. The cold was intense, and she could feel its bite even through the thick layers of her snowsuit. And while the fur-lined boots were indeed much warmer than her hiking boots, she wasn't sure her throbbing feet would survive an entire night in these conditions.

"Hmm." His mouth was again in that thin line of determination. "If they have other men, or other teams tracking you, they might try to block all roads out of here. Our best chance is to ride the hidden trails through the forest and get to Jokkmokk via the back way."

"Okay, let's do that," she replied brightly. How could she have doubted him? Of course he would have a plan B.

"It's an hour's ride through the freezing dark. Are you up for that?"

Did she have any choice? Briefly, she thought about her hands and feet. At the moment, the adrenaline was still pumping through her veins, keeping her warm, but when that vanished, how would she feel then? She would just have to endure, so she nodded and pulled her balaclava down over her face.

Jacob continued to stare at her for a few more moments, as if weighing up her capacity to keep going. She stared steadily back at him, knowing that only her eyes would show, but she gave him nothing but determination. The last thing he needed was to worry about her. He was the only one who could get them safely to town, and she required his full concentration on the path ahead, not worrying about her. At least Jacob's body had shielded her from most of the icy wind as they sped through the wintry night; he had no nice warm body in front of him to stave off the freezing air whipping past them. Despite his claiming to be used to these conditions, perhaps she should be more worried about him.

"Right. Hang on tight," he said, turning his head forward. "I'll get us there as quickly as I can."

CHAPTER SIX

Jacob was so cold he could barely swing his leg over the seat to dismount. For the past hour, he'd been so focused on getting them safely into town, he hadn't registered his own discomfort. But now they'd stopped, he sensed how close his body was to succumbing to the freezing temperatures. But he still had a job to do and a woman to protect. *Faan*, he hoped she hadn't turned into a frozen icicle on the back of the machine. He'd halted every ten minutes to check on her, and each time she'd stubbornly insisted she was fine, but he knew she must be at least as cold as he was. Their best chance of survival was escaping out of the snow and into shelter, and so he'd kept going, always on the lookout for any pursuit from behind. He'd been right about the two guys being on foot, because nothing eventuated.

Steadying himself on the slippery ground, he turned and offered a hand to Nikki, helping her to step off the machine. She moved tentatively, testing each step before committing to placing a boot on the icy snow. Swaying, she gripped his arm and released a hiss of pain. Her feet were probably still sore, and this extra time out in the cold wouldn't have helped. At any other moment, he would've scooped her up in his arms like he had back in the hut, but he didn't trust his chilled-to-the-bone legs to hold her. Her balaclava was covered in icicles where the water vapor from her warm breath had frozen solid, and as she pulled it up, icy shards rained down the front of her suit.

"Where are we?" she asked through chattering teeth.

"At a friend's place." There was no designated safe house in this tiny town in the middle of northern Sweden. The nearest secure location was in Luleå, over two hours' drive away in good weather. Petar would be surprised when Jacob knocked on his door, but Jacob was counting on the fact that he'd let them in with no questions asked, even though it was getting late.

"We'll be safe here for a little while," he added, putting an arm around her shoulder to help steady her as they made their slow way up the path toward the back door, silently thanking Petar for his diligence in keeping the way shoveled and clear of snow.

Whoever was after them might well follow their snowmobile tracks to the outskirts of Jokkmokk, but after that, he'd ridden on the recently graded dirt streets, and even on some of the bitumen roads. The rubber tracks would be ruined, but it'd made them practically untraceable. Barring going around and knocking on every door of every house in the town, the hitmen wouldn't know where they were holed up. Yet.

Nikki stumbled up the last step onto the porch, and he clung more tightly to her, pulling her into his body to steady her. Even with the bulky snowsuit on, she was small beneath his hand, her shoulders thin and shaking. The same wave of protectiveness that'd hit him back in the hut surged through his gut again. He wasn't certain why, but he'd do almost anything to make sure she stayed safe. She didn't deserve to be targeted, not like this. It was clear her universe had just been turned upside down, none of it her fault, but she kept going like a trooper, not giving in to despair or fatigue, and he respected her for her strength.

With his free hand, he knocked on the door. They waited for many long moments before it opened a crack, and Petar's familiar face squinted at them through the chink.

Jacob tugged off his knit cap. "It's me, Jacob," he said in a low voice. They might've already raised some wary watchfulness in the nearby neighboring houses by arriving on a noisy snowmobile in the dead of night; they didn't need a loud altercation outside the house to raise any more concern. Jacob registered surprise in his friend's eyes for a split second, but it soon changed to genuine anxiety.

"Jacob, mate, what are you doing out there in the cold?" His astute gaze flicked to the woman nestled beneath Jacob's arm. He wasn't about to offer her name, not out here where anyone might hear them. Instead, he turned to Nikki and said, "This is Petar. He's a good friend from my school days." Nikki looked up at Petar and gave a wan smile. One look at her face and Petar's welcoming grin shifted to a frown of consternation.

"Come in, come in. You need to get warm." He swept the door wide open and beckoned them in, taking Nikki's elbow when she stumbled into him. His friend had clearly been in bed, answering the door in flannel pajamas, his dark hair sleep mussed, but he never missed a beat as he led her to a bench seat in the mudroom, bending down to help her remove her boots without even having to be asked, leaving Jacob to tend to his own gear. He dropped his white backpack off his chest, and it landed with a thump on the floor. It was his go-bag, containing everything he might need if he had to flee in a hurry. Carrying the bag in front of him had given him some more, much-needed protection from the elements, as well as keeping it out of Nikki's way.

Jacob was silently grateful that Petar was able to sense

Nikki's distress and jump right in to help. He hoped that Petar's current on-again-off-again girlfriend, Ingola, wasn't sleeping over tonight. The fewer witnesses they had, the better. No one spoke as they disrobed, and even when Petar spotted Nikki's swollen feet, he kept his comments to himself, for which Jacob was again appreciative.

Jacob had met Petar when they'd both been eight years old, on Jacob's first day at the local elementary school in Jokkmokk. Jacob had only recently moved to Sweden from America with his mother after his parents' marriage had broken down, and was suffering severe cultural shock. When his love-struck mom had run off to the United States to marry his father, she'd left family and tradition behind without so much as blinking an eye. But once the relationship ended, she realized what she'd given up to follow a man across the world—the culture and traditions her kids were now missing out on—and all she wanted was to return home so Jacob and his sister, Rikka, could learn about their Sámi heritage. At first, the siblings were appalled, struggling to fit in after leaving everything familiar and starting a new life. Jacob had stumbled into the classroom of this unfamiliar and scary world, shaking and mute, feeling homesick and lost. But the teacher had allocated him a seat next to this tall, gangly boy, and Petar had smiled at him. When the teacher had turned away, Petar had whispered, "Look at this." He'd opened his mouth and proudly pushed at a wobbly tooth that was hanging on by the merest of threads. "It's disgusting, isn't it? Do you want to help me pull it out at lunchtime?" Jacob had been relieved to hear Petar speak English; most of his relatives only spoke the local dialect, and Jacob often had no idea what they were saying to him.

Jacob and Petar had been unbreakable friends ever since. They'd stayed in touch, even after Jacob had left town to start his training as a cop, while Petar stayed and took a job at the nearby pulp mill. Jacob's mother still lived in Jokkmokk amongst the rest of her side of the family, and so he had plenty of reasons to come and visit, and every time he did he made sure to catch up with his best mate. Petar had even been the one to introduce Jacob to his current girlfriend, Freya, one of Ingola's good friends, and they had been on a couple of double dates whenever the pair visited Luleå.

Jacob winced as he thought of Freya. It was another reason he was glad Ingola wasn't staying over tonight; he didn't want to face her accusing stares. Jacob was still loath to commit to Freya, even though they'd been dating for nearly a year. But Freya had hinted that she wanted more, and Jacob had been actively avoiding the issue, and recently had even been avoiding Freya. He'd only seen her twice in the past month, and both times had been more of a booty call than anything else. He was acting like a dick, and he knew it; he knew Ingola would have given him a piece of her mind if she were here. And he would deserve it. But right now, the last thing he needed was thoughts of how badly he was treating Freya screwing with his head.

Jacob glanced over to see that Petar had helped Nikki out of her boots and snowsuit and was now assisting her to her feet, taking her by the elbow to help her hobble into the kitchen, glancing back over his shoulder at Jacob with a single raised eyebrow before they disappeared through the door. Jacob gave a weary nod of appreciation for his friend's help, still struggling to undo the zipper on his own suit; his fingers were numb and almost useless. At least the snowsuits kept their clothes underneath dry, so there was no need to drag off wet garments. A few minutes later, Jacob snagged Nikki's backpack that Petar had hung on a hook in the mudroom, along with his own, and followed them into the blessedly warm kitchen. He found Nikki seated at a small table beneath a window, a mug of steaming hot chocolate in front of her. She glanced up at him, blue eyes shadowed with fatigue, as he placed the bag at her feet.

"Yours is on the counter," Petar pointed to another mug next to the stove. "I'm going to get her some warm socks and a blanket." He was gone before Jacob could say it was a great idea. He hunkered down beside Nikki so his face was level with hers, groaning as his numb legs protested at the movement.

"How are you?" he asked, scanning her pale features for signs of hypothermia. Her lovely countenance told him everything he needed to know. Her cheeks were ashen, but her teeth had stopped chattering, and while the lines around her eyes were drawn with tiredness, there remained a tiny spark in them that lifted his heart. Her long, blonde hair was a snarl of tangles where it'd flapped free below the balaclava, making her look even more girlish and vulnerable.

"Better now. Your friend makes the best chocolate. He may well have just saved my life." She gave an appreciative slurp and then licked her lips, drawing his gaze down to her mouth. Her lips were recovering some of their pink color, and he watched, fascinated, as she swept a drop of chocolate from the corner of her mouth with her tongue, pulling it inside where she savored the taste. Fixated, he could do nothing but stare at her lips. He could barely believe it, but even now, half-frozen and running for his life, all he could think about was what it'd be like to kiss those lips. He'd wanted to taste her back at his hut, but now the urge was even greater, the ridiculous notion that they'd just escaped from a dire situation driving him to want to capture the moment right now, while he still could. Nikki's breath hitched as she caught him staring at her mouth, and she bit her bottom lip, her gaze locking onto his. Something fiery flared in the depths of her ocean-blue eyes. God, she was sexy, and so damn tempting. With the face of an angel, so innocent, yet there was a core of steel and passion coursing just below the surface; he could feel it.

"What are you…?" Her voice was a whisper.

What indeed? He closed his eyes, trying to break the spell. But her fingers found his cheek, rasping against his three-day growth, and —

A door banged behind him and Jacob sprang to his feet, backing away from Nikki just as Petar bustled into the kitchen, arms full of blankets. "Here, this one is for you." His friend tossed a gray fleece blanket in Jacob's direction, then bent over Nikki, reverentially draping another blanket around her shoulders. Jacob turned to face the countertop, pretending to untangle the thick material and wrap it around his shoulders, while he gave the bulge in his pants a chance to retreat. What had he been thinking? That was the second time he'd come close to kissing her. He retrieved his mug, his glacial hands welcoming the warmth of the hot drink into his palms. A coffee drinker, he screwed up his nose as he took a sip of the sweet, creamy liquid, but was quietly surprised. The last occasion he'd drunk hot chocolate had been when he was a kid, but Nikki was right; this was damn good stuff. He could feel the sugar reviving him already.

Petar was now on his knees, helping Nikki pull a woolen sock gently over her sore foot. Jacob took a chair next to Nikki, giving his friend a hard look as he continued to fuss around her. A surprising sliver of jealousy wormed its way through his gut as he watched Petar tend to her. Not something he was used to, especially when he was on the job. But he seemed unable to control that hint of possessiveness when it came to this woman, and he wanted to growl at Petar to get away from her.

Petar must've felt the vibe of Jacob's growing ire, and rose to his feet with a small frown in Jacob's direction, leaving Nikki to pull on the other sock by herself. Dragging out a seat on the other side of the table and stretching out his long, pajama-clad legs, Petar said, "So, are you going to tell me what's happening?"

Nikki stopped, the mug half-way to her mouth, and shared a look with Jacob, uncertainty in her gaze.

"Do you mind if we close the curtains?" Jacob asked. It was a Swedish tradition to leave a small lamp burning in the window, possibly stemming from the belief it would send out its golden light like a beacon in the snow, to help guide people lost in a blizzard home. Usually the drapes also remained open, but tonight Jacob needed privacy.

Jacob could feel Petar's growing puzzlement, but he got up and did as Jacob requested, twitching the curtains shut and making sure not even a chink of light was visible. He sat down again and stared pointedly at Jacob.

"It's okay, we can talk in front of Petar. I trust him with my life," he assured Nikki. Petar was Sámi, like himself. There was an unwritten code; they would do anything to protect their community and the people in it. Once his mother had brought him and his sister back to rejoin the family, even though Jacob may have moved away to join the police force, he would always be Sámi in the clan's eyes.

Nikki's gaze darted between the two men, narrowing when it came to rest on Jacob. "Well, I guess I trust him with my life then too."

Petar gave a grunt and sat up straighter, but to his credit, said nothing.

Jacob quickly outlined the day's events, starting with his phone call from the deputy commissioner and ending with their harrowing flight on the snowmobile. All the while, Nikki watched him with those big, trusting, blue eyes of hers.

"Shit. That's intense," Petar replied when Jacob stopped speaking. "That must've been tough even for a hardened police officer." He switched his gaze over to Nikki. "But it must've been damn scary for you."

She merely nodded, perhaps not wanting to relive it all over again.

"Yeah, intense is one word for it," Jacob butted in, dragging his friend's attention back to himself. "Look, mate, I hope I haven't brought trouble to your door, but we had nowhere else to go. I mean, I couldn't go to my mother's because—"

Petar held up his hand. "Of course you shouldn't involve your family; I completely understand. You know you're always welcome here, no matter what issues you might drag in behind you," he added with a cheeky grin. "And who doesn't love a bit of drama now and then? But you know I can look after myself, so don't you worry about that." Petar sobered quickly as he spoke. "And you also know I will keep an eye on your family, so don't worry about them either."

Yes, he could look after himself, Jacob knew, and it was one reason he'd come straight here. Petar was tough, a true Northern Sami man. He could hunt, survive in the wilderness, and even kill a man if that was ever necessary. Then there was the fact that the clans would protect Petar. This was one unbreakable little community that looked after each other and had each other's backs. If the gunmen turned up, they would soon be run out of town, or worse; they were the ones who should be afraid. But the sooner Jacob could be out of here, the sooner Petar would be out of immediate danger.

Which led him to his next request. "I need to borrow a car," Jacob said flatly. He knew he was asking a lot. In this small town, a vehicle was essential to get around. There was no public transport to speak of, except buses that infrequently traveled the main roads between the remote communities, out to Luleå on the coast, or to the larger cities further south. Petar's job as the manager at the local pulp mill, which was fifteen miles out of town, meant that he used his car every day to drive to work. Jacob would leave his friend in the lurch by calling in this favor. Petar had a snowmobile, of course, but those were for emergencies only in freezing weather such as this. Apart from stealing a car, however, he couldn't think of any alternatives. They needed to get to Luleå in a hurry, and a vehicle was the only way to do it.

Petar scrubbed a hand across his forehead. "I was afraid you were going to say that," he said with a sigh. "Of course you can have my Volvo."

"What about my hire car? Can't we use that?" Nikki interrupted. It was the first time she'd spoken since Jacob had started his story. Jacob had watched the color slowly come back to her face, her skin losing that pale, translucent look from her exposure to the freezing temperatures. The heat of Petar's kitchen and his hot chocolate were doing the trick to revive her. Jacob felt a stab of regret that he'd been the one to inflict such suffering on her. If he could've kept her warm and safe in his hut until morning, he would've. They'd had no choice but to flee, however, and he hoped with all his heart that her hands and feet weren't permanently scarred from this experience. Which reminded him he should take another peek soon.

"They'll most likely be on the lookout for your vehicle," Jacob said softly.

"Oh." Comprehension dawned on her face.

"I'll arrange for someone to get it back to the hire company in the next few days once you're safe." Then as an afterthought, he turned to Petar and added, "Can you please let Andreas Eriksson know he doesn't need to collect Nikki from his hut tomorrow. Tell him as little as possible about the reasons why," Jacob added.

"Andreas will keep his mouth shut; don't worry about him," Petar confirmed. Jacob nodded, trusting Petar's assessment. While Jacob had moved away from Jokkmokk over ten years ago, Petar had remained embedded in the community and the Sámi way of life, and in this small town everyone knew everybody else.

"Good." That was one more thing Jacob didn't have to worry about. But a quick glance in Nikki's direction reminded him he was still worried about her. If she needed proper treatment, he might have to alter his plan substantially. "Do you mind if I take a quick look at your feet?" He gestured below the table, and Nikki's face became pensive.

"Hmm, okay," she agreed. "But if it's bad news, I'm not sure I want to know."

If it was bad news, they probably should get her to a hospital, but he kept that to himself as he kneeled before her and gently peeled Petar's large sock down her leg and over her ankle to reveal her toes. They were still red, but seemed to have lost some of their puffiness, which was a good sign. The little pinky toe was also regaining some color, not white and lifeless anymore. At least his specially tailored snow boots had made sure they didn't receive more damage from the cold on their flight on the snowmobile. After checking the other foot and finding it much the same as the first, he let out a relieved gust of air.

"I take it my toes have passed the test," she said, trying to peer past him and get a look at her feet.

"Yes, they'll still be sore for a day or so, but there should be no permanent damage," he replied, pulling the sock back on. Her feet were as petite and elegant as the rest of her. He'd never given much thought to feet before; certainly never considered them as beautiful or alluring. But even red-tinged and puffy, hers appealed to him like no others had ever done. He could imagine them draped in his lap as they both lay relaxing on the couch, him massaging the strain of the day away, running his hands over the curves of her heel and up her slim ankles until…

There he went again, letting his libido get the better of him.

He stood a little too quickly and retreated until his rear end met the countertop. Time for a quick change of topic. Back to the business at hand. "Do you have access to the data your team collected? I mean, did you share your documents with your colleagues?" he asked, his tone gruffer than he intended. He'd meant to ask this back when the deputy commissioner mentioned the missing laptops, but the hitmen had appeared before he'd had a chance to pose the question.

Nikki looked up, confusion clouding her face.

"It's the data they're after," he clarified. "Even if they get rid of you, if that information gets out into the world, they're still screwed." Surely the same idea must've occurred to her too?

Glancing down at her laptop bag on the floor, he saw the moment when comprehension arrived and she sat up straighter. She answered him slowly. "We all maintained separate records on our individual laptops. We were all researching different aspects of the pollution. Mine was specifically microplastic contamination of the water, checking water quality, that sort of thing. While Tammy was looking at the effect on the environment of the larger plastic waste, such as how it affected sediment load. And Antoine was looking at how plastic waste is entering the marine food chain, and the harm it's causing, especially in larger aquatic animals as it accumulates up the chain."

Jacob's heart sank at the news. That all sounded impossibly convoluted and complicated. But Nikki sat up a little straighter, slitting her eyes at him.

"Tammy set up a shared Dropbox. The plan was to upload our documents at the end of every day to make sure we lost nothing." Nikki pursed her lips and made a face. "Of course, being imperfect humans, we were always too busy to do that most days. But…" Nikki paused, and the room went silent as she sorted through her thoughts. "I uploaded my raw data on the day we finished our research, because I knew I'd be off-grid for the next week. Back then, I never checked to see if Tammy and Antoine had done the same." She glanced at him, hope burgeoning in her eyes.

"You think they might've done it too?" he asked.

"Yes. All I need is a Wi-Fi connection, and I could check and see." Animation made her face come alight, and Jacob almost lost his breath at how beautiful she was.

Both of them swung their gazes in Petar's direction, and he held his hands up as if in surrender. "First you wanted my Volvo and now you want my Wi-Fi. What next?" he quipped, but his face became serious when neither of them smiled at his attempt to lighten the mood. "Yeah, I have Wi-Fi. Let me get you the password," he grumbled as he got out of his chair. Jacob owed his friend big time for all his help. Without him, they might still be stuck out in the cold on a snowmobile. He would repay his debt soon once this was all over.

CHAPTER SEVEN

Nikki gazed ahead through the windshield, not really registering the dark, treacherous road unfolding in front of them as they hurtled toward Luleå in Petar's Volvo. The car was old, and battered; a few of the door panels showed signs of rust, but at least the heating worked, and Petar had assured them it was reliable. Jacob drove, his capable hands guiding the car skillfully across the snowy highway. She trusted he knew what he was doing, and so, sitting beside him in the passenger seat with not a lot else to do but stare out the window, she had time to think. And her thoughts were locked in a loop, going over and over all that'd occurred today. So much had happened, her mind was struggling to keep up. She could barely believe Jacob had entered her life less than twelve hours ago and turned everything upside down in an instant.

Twelve hours since he'd burst into her sauna and found her naked.

Oh, gosh, she'd forgotten all about that in the ensuing period of madness. But now, a delayed sense of embarrassment washed through her. She remembered standing in front of him, desperately trying to cover herself. But then as the memory became clearer, she also noted that

74

he'd stared at her blankly, as if he was gazing at a statue made of stone, not a living, breathing woman formed from flesh and blood. Most men would've leered at her, or at the very least let their gaze wander the length of her body. Was he superhuman? Was she no longer attractive to the opposite sex? Or, was it *he* hadn't found *her* attractive? She knew she'd allowed herself to get on the skinny side, but she'd put on a few pounds in the last two weeks, which rounded out her curves a little more. A shred of doubt wormed its way into her mind; he hadn't liked what he'd seen. It was pathetic, but the idea stung more than she'd like to admit.

Until she remembered how he'd looked at her mouth back at Petar's house, as if he'd wanted to ravage her, as if he'd wanted to draw her to him and kiss her until neither of them could breathe. She hadn't been imagining that, because she'd felt the heat of his gaze and her body had reacted to the desire so clearly burning in his hazel eyes, sending an answering spike of heat through her core.

It was more than a little confusing.

Was there something between them, or was she just fantasizing? She felt a certain pull when he was around, a deep uncharted need forming low down in her belly whenever he looked at her. Some might call it chemistry. Craving, even. But that was ridiculous; she barely knew the man. And she definitely didn't believe in love at first sight. She was a scientist who believed in facts and figures, not absurd romantic notions.

"What's going on in that head of yours?" Jacob asked, startling her when his voice broke into her musings. For a stupid second she wondered if he could read minds.

"Oh, ah…nothing important," she replied. But her tone wasn't as breezy and uncaring as she'd hoped.

"You've been staring out that window for the past half an hour without saying a word," he chided. "There's not nothing going on in there, I can hear the cogs whirring from here." He turned his head to give her a quick smile, that unexpected dimple appearing before he returned his focus back to the road.

"I was just sorting through everything that's happened today," she admitted after a moment's pause. Maybe it'd be better to talk things over, get them out in the open. Especially if she could sort out how he felt about her and get rid of this buzzing uncertainty from her head, then she could conceivably move on to the more important stuff, like how they were going to survive the next few hours and days. "Starting back at Andreas' hut, when you…" She stopped, not sure how to phrase her thoughts out loud. "I just wanted to say thank you for not…" She coughed and started again, hoping he didn't notice the flush climbing her cheeks. "For being a gentleman about catching me naked in the sauna. The whole thing was traumatic enough without you…you know, ogling me. I've never done anything like that before, and…"

She trailed off as he let out a bark of laughter, surprising her so much that she turned to gape at his profile, lit by the ghostly glow of the dashboard lights. Why did he think seeing her in the nude was funny? Oh gosh, she suddenly wished those words back into her mouth. Now he thought she was being precious about the whole thing.

"I'm Swedish, you know," he said, as if that told her everything she needed to know. Did he mean he was Swedish and so was used to seeing other women naked in the sauna? Or was he implying that Swedish men were renowned for suppressing their emotions, their faces impassive, and not ogling women's bodies?

"Okay," she replied, keeping her gaze fixed on the windscreen. He hadn't given her an answer to her unasked question, but she wasn't about to pry any deeper because this was becoming more humiliating by the moment.

Jacob flashed her a quick, unreadable glance. "But don't for a second think that you weren't worth looking at. I was doing my job, that's all. You are a beautiful woman, Nikita."

"Oh." His soft words sent a flood of warmth through her veins. She liked the sound of her full name on his lips. Like a caress. No one but her mother called her Nikita. But out of his mouth, it made her feel special, as if he took her seriously. "Thank you," she added belatedly, not sure how to respond to such a compliment.

At least now she knew she wasn't just imagining this *thing* between them. But to her annoyance, the knowledge did nothing to relieve her preoccupation. In fact, it made it worse. Because now she wanted to know more, wanted to find out what it was really like to kiss him. To see if the chemistry burned as brightly as she suspected it did.

No, she needed to refocus, get her head back on straight and stop mooning after a man she barely knew.

Nikki forced her brain to think about their predicament instead. Her thoughts returned to Petar's house, where she'd linked into his Wi-Fi and, after a few moments of agitated waiting for the website to load, had thrust her fist triumphantly into the air. Both Tammy and Antoine had uploaded their data to the Dropbox. The feeling of relief had been so intense, she'd jumped up and hugged Jacob, forgetting all about her sore feet. It seemed like such a win after everything that'd gone wrong today. Like a tiny stroke of redemption for her friends.

She'd downloaded the info onto her computer and then sent a quick email to Russell Morgan with it all attached, telling him to back it up and guard it with his life. At least now, even if those two brilliant scientists were no longer here, someone else could carry on the undertaking they'd started.

She would do it. She would take that data and turn it into a weapon. Aim it straight at that dirty corporation and its henchmen and bring them down.

She just needed to stay alive long enough to do it.

* * *

Nikki's head snapped up, and her eyes flew open. "What… Where…?"

"It's okay. You fell asleep." Jacob leaned in the door of the car, saying, "I stopped for gas and snacks; figured you were asleep and I didn't want to wake you. We've still got over an hour to go before we hit Luleå, and I'm starving."

"Oh." She scrubbed a hand across her brow, trying to work some sense into her comatose brain. Harsh spotlights beat down through the windshield, and she blinked in the brightness, focusing on the gas pumps beside the car and the small, brightly lit shop to the right.

"You're cute when you sleep, you know," he said, folding his long legs into the vehicle as he pulled the door shut behind him.

"I beg your pardon?" What did he mean by that?

"It's okay, you weren't snoring or anything," he said with a mischievous grin. "Just cute." Was Jacob flirting with her? If he was… Her mind was too muzzy to process that properly. Perhaps he was picking up on their earlier conversation, where he'd admitted that he thought she was beautiful? And now he was adding *cute* to the mix. She should tell him she considered him pretty damn hot too, but she wasn't sure where all these intriguing thoughts were leading. They'd been thrown together by a whirlwind of circumstance, and they might be torn apart just as fast. Once he delivered her to his superiors in Luleå, she might never see him again. The idea pained her more than she liked to admit. So perhaps flirting should just be left off the table. If they couldn't act on any of their feelings, what was the point? Gosh darn it, this was all too much to work out at one a.m. in the morning.

Before she could form any sort of reasonable reply,

however, he handed over a paper bag, then started the car, easing it onto the highway, and they picked up speed.

"There's water and candy bars in there," he prompted when she continued to stare at him without looking into the bag now sitting in her lap. "While Petar's hot chocolate was reinvigorating, well…" He gave a shrug as if to say it wasn't enough. She understood that they'd already imposed on Petar's hospitality sufficiently that night, as well as taking away his only means of transport, and the last thing Jacob was going to ask for was provisions to stock the car.

She was hungry too, but when she opened the bag and looked inside, she gave a groan of censure. Inside lay the bane of her life.

"What's up?" He asked, pursing his lips in confusion. "Did I get the wrong chocolate?"

Nikki reached in and held one of the two bottles of water aloft. "Single use plastic," she accused. When he looked at her blankly, she continued, "Do you know how many of these are floating in the ocean right now? Clogging up the beaches and waterways, and being ingested by marine mammals?"

"No." Uncertainty edged his words, but she would not let him get away with this. Nikki had made it her mission to educate people about their polluting habits, and just because Jacob had saved her life—multiple times—didn't mean he was exempt from her reprimands.

"I make a point never to buy single-use plastic items," she said. "There are always alternatives, like buying in glass or metal containers, or taking your own water bottle. And if there aren't, well, you go thirsty. Or drink from a tap."

"Really?" He seemed genuinely perplexed, glancing away from the darkened highway to shoot a look at her. "But sometimes you don't have a choice," he argued.

"Yes," she replied. "Everyone always has a choice. If even one less piece of plastic discarded into landfill might help to save the life of a turtle who mistakes it for food, or a shearwater chick grow to adulthood because its been fed real fish instead of fragments of plastic, then I'll do it."

"Okay. I don't disagree with you." He shifted uncomfortably in his seat. "But I guess it's not always top of mind with me."

"Well, it should be," she said hotly, indignation getting the better of her. Why were people so unconcerned about what was happening to their planet? Like it was someone else's problem to fix, not theirs. She was working up a good head of steam now. "It's all about education," she went on. "Educating the government as well as individuals. If we can educate the consumer to want more; to want something that's sustainable and good for the world instead of something that's the cheapest option, then all those money-centric companies will have to make a change."

"I agree," Jacob replied, his brow furrowed with concern. "And I'll try to do better next time," he promised. "You're feisty when you get fired up." That dimple was back in his cheek, and Nikki's annoyance deflated in an instant.

She couldn't help but return his smile. "Sorry," she said. "Lecture over. For now," she added with a grin.

Now she was wide awake and feeling a little foolish, knowing that if she'd achieved nothing else with her schoolmarmish tone, she'd poured cold water all over his attempts at flirting with her. They drove in silence for the next few miles, Jacob quietly munching on his candy bar and taking guilty swigs from his bottle, while she stared out the window.

The rumblings of her stomach eventually compelled her to retrieve a nut bar from the bag and take a few gulps of water from the nasty plastic bottle. She'd make sure that at least for the rest of the duration of this trip, they refilled these bottles rather than discarding them and buying more. It was the least they could do.

Drawing a deep breath, she turned to look at Jacob just as he covered his mouth to hide a yawn. It reminded her how exhausted she was, so fatigued that her brief nap had done nothing to assuage her need for sleep. Being a cop, he would be more used to this kind of adrenaline-fueled stuff, but he must be tired too. Now that she was really looking at him, she could make out the dark smudges under his eyes. A stab of guilt hit her in the guts; he was carrying the weight of their worries, and here she was sleeping while he drove through the night, then attacking him about his choice of drink container when he tried to ease his thirst.

She traced his profile as he stared through the windshield. Long, straight nose, dark lashes ringing his piercing hazel eyes, and sable hair short on the sides, but left longer on top to curl enticingly over his forehead. Firm mouth and defined cheekbones partially hidden behind his short, neat beard that made him look even more rugged. He was so damn sexy, Nikki's fingers twitched with wanting to reach out and stroke the side of his face, to smooth away the lines of worry lining his brow.

If he was going to drive all the way, then the least she could do was talk to him to keep him awake. Searching for something to open the conversation with that didn't have to do with death or hitmen or plastic bottles, she started with the first thing that sprang to mind.

"So, tell me, what's it like growing up in a tiny country town in the middle of northern Sweden?" she asked.

"What?" He swung his tired gaze around to meet hers.

"I grew up in a typical American town, with typical American parents and went to a typical American school," she said. Not completely true, but that wasn't the point right now. "Your life here is very different from mine. I'd like to learn about it if you don't mind talking."

He shrugged those nice, broad shoulders and said, "Sure, why not." Then, he recounted the story of how he'd met Petar on his first day at school and how they'd bonded over his disgustingly wobbly tooth. He went on to tell her about his family and his Sámi heritage, of which he was very proud. It surprised her to find out he'd been born in America and only moved back here when his parents had divorced. But at least that explained why he spoke such good English. His life in Jokkmokk appeared almost idyllic, the years of his adolescence spent hiking in summer and skiing in winter, learning how to muster the great herds of reindeer owned by his extended family, hunting and foraging for wild food while they spent weeks or months out in the wilderness. It was all so different from her own in academia, which seemed sheltered in comparison. Admittedly, she'd also taken part in many field trips to some rugged and isolated areas, and at least she shared that love of the outdoors with him, even if she didn't posses the same survival techniques he did.

Time flew past as she listened to Jacob talk, and she told him a little about her life in Seattle in return. Sooner than expected, street lamps lit the road ahead, and Jacob slowed the car to a more suburban pace. Luleå looked to be a substantial city, and while deserted at this time of night, would most likely be buzzing during the day.

"Where are we headed now?" she asked wearily, tired of all this subterfuge. She just wanted a warm bed and a soft pillow and to forget this was all happening for a few hours.

"Polismyndigheten i Norrbotten," he replied. "The main police hub for the area," he amended with a smile. "The deputy commissioner will most likely be waiting there to talk to us." She knew him well enough by now to understand his smile was forced; he was keeping it bright for her sake. There was something about meeting this deputy commissioner that was weighing on Jacob.

"Even at this time of the morning?"

"Yes, he's expecting us. I kept him updated on our travel plans."

"Oh, goodie." But she wasn't sure it was good. It didn't sound like a bed and a soft pillow were anywhere in her near future. She would be secure at police headquarters; no one would be bold enough to assassinate her there. But would the deputy commissioner be able to help her? And did it mean that her time with Jacob was nearly over? Would he be sent away now that his job of saving her from immediate peril was over? Her lips formed a thin line of disappointment as despondency settled heavy in her stomach.

CHAPTER EIGHT

Jacob lifted his chin and drew in a soft breath before he raised his hand and rapped on the door. He wasn't looking forward to this meeting. Hoped that he wouldn't have to confront the deputy commissioner until after the inquisition was over and they had cleared him and Mårten of all wrongdoing. As it was, Deputy Commissioner Staaf would be more belligerent than normal because he'd had no choice but to use Jacob for this mission, and that man hated to be backed into a corner. The gall of having to call on Jacob—who had already come to his notice on more than one occasion for all the wrong reasons because of his tendency not to do things strictly by the book—would not sit well with the man. But Nikki's safety trumped all of his feelings of apprehension, and he would just have to face the deputy commissioner with head held high.

"Come in," a voice commanded, and Jacob opened the door, schooling his features into an impassive blank slate. This office belonged to Jacob's boss, Chief Superintendent Rydberg. But the deputy commissioner had appropriated it for his impromptu late-night visit. Chief Rydberg had met them at the front desk, bleary-eyed and hiding a yawn, not happy to have been pulled out of bed in the wee hours of the morning. But he couldn't very well refuse the deputy commissioner, especially when it was one of his officers conducting this poorly planned and highly clandestine operation at the deputy commissioner's behest, even if he was on suspension.

The chief had given Jacob an understanding pat on the shoulder and told him he would talk to him after he'd seen the deputy commissioner. He was more sympathetic when it came to Jacob and Mårten's failed mission than the deputy commissioner, who was a stickler for the rules. As their commanding officer, Rydberg worked closely with them and knew they were two of his best officers. Knew that both men had put themselves in the line of fire to save Tristan, who had disobeyed a direct order. But his opinion mattered less than the deputy commissioners at this moment in time, so Jacob straightened his spine and lifted his chin.

"Inspector Utsi." Runar glared at Jacob through thick, black-rimmed glasses. He was a bull of a man with a neck as sturdy as a tree trunk and a full head of buzz-cut, iron-gray hair. If anyone looked the part of a police deputy commissioner, it was Runar Staaf; he'd earned his reputation as a take-no-prisoners type of guy.

"Biträdande Poliskommissarie Staaf," Jacob responded, standing to attention in front of the desk. Nikki had followed him in, still hobbling on her sore feet, and he was acutely aware of her slight frame right next to him. "I'd like to introduce Dr. Nikita Winter in person." He allowed himself one quick glance in Nikki's direction.

"Pleased to meet you, Deputy Commissioner." Nikki reached a hand across the table, taking Runar by surprise so that he had to shove his chair back in a hurry. Jacob smiled inwardly at her forthrightness; American women had such an air of self-confidence and weren't afraid to speak their minds.

"I'm glad to see that you got here safely and in one piece," he responded. But Jacob didn't miss the slight side-eye Runar sent in his direction. Calm. He needed to stay calm. The deputy commissioner was well within his rights to doubt Jacob's abilities right now. He just hoped that Runar chose not to bring up his failings in front of Nikki. "Please take a seat." Runar gestured to the two chairs on the opposite of the desk.

Nikki pulled out the one closest to her and, gritting his teeth, he dragged out the other one and took a seat.

"Yes, I'm unharmed thanks to the heroic efforts of your wonderful inspector here," Nikki said, giving the deputy commissioner her brightest smile. "If it weren't for him, I'd most likely be lying dead in that holiday hut right now. So thank you for sending him." If Jacob didn't know better, he might've thought that Nikki was turning on the charm offensive. As if she could feel the tension in the air, and was doing her best to relieve it. Jacob had already ascertained that Nikki was a beautiful woman, but even armed with this knowledge, he was still almost blinded by the charisma of her wide, beaming smile. When he glanced at Runar, he was gratified to notice that the cool, battle-weary deputy commissioner wasn't immune to her allure either, as he blinked owlishly at her for a few seconds, seeming unable to form a coherent answer.

Recovering his demeanor, Runar cleared his throat and said, "Hmm, yes, well." He frowned and pushed his glasses further up his nose. "Inspector Utsi is very good at what he does," he replied, barely able to keep the grudging tone out of his voice. "Usually," he added, switching his dark gaze toward Jacob. "Anyway, I'm glad you escaped the hitmen. I believe there were two of them?"

"Yes, sir. And they were shooting to kill," Jacob confirmed. "Clearly, the desire to pretend Nikki's death was from accidental causes has been replaced by the urgency of wanting their last target dead."

"Clearly," the deputy commissioner echoed. "I've sent a team to the area to trace the two hitmen. They found their snowmobile tracks on the road out to your holiday hut, Dr. Winter. But they ditched the machines in Jokkmokk and traded them for a car, and our team lost track of them after that." Runar lifted his head and stared hawk-like at Nikki, his professional demeanor back in place. "But do not concern yourself, Dr. Winter, we will find them soon. And in the meantime, we won't let them get anywhere near you. We have every available officer in the vicinity on the lookout for them. You're safe here."

"Thank you, Deputy Commissioner." Nikki copied Runar's serious tone, her heart-shaped face tilted toward him earnestly. "That's heartening to hear."

"I've arranged somewhere for you to spend the night," Runar continued in his officious manner. "You'll be under twenty-four-hour guard. And I'm personally looking into an airplane to get you out of Sweden and out of harm's way as quickly as possible," he added.

Wow, that was news to Jacob. Runar was taking this whole thing extremely seriously, and it made Jacob wonder why. This thing must have international repercussions, and Runar was perhaps getting pressure from higher up to sort this out promptly, especially if he was expediting Nikki out of Sweden as soon as possible. Maybe it was as simple as him merely wanting her out of the country so she was no longer his problem.

"Thank you," Nikki finally replied. "That...sounds wonderful." Was Jacob imagining it, or did she just shoot him a look under lowered lashes? What was she up to now? "Will Jac—Inspector Utsi—continue to be part of my protection team?" Runar began to shake his head and opened his mouth to reply, but Nikki jumped in before he could say anything more. "I'm only asking because I feel safe with him. Without him, I don't think I would've been able to make that terrible trek through the snow and ice to get away from those dangerous hitmen. And then when I thought I had frostbite, he treated me with such care and compassion. Always respectful and professional, of course," she added quickly. "And, well…I trust him, and I'm not sure I could trust anyone else," she finished, lifting pleading blue eyes to the deputy commissioner's face.

Wow, it'd take a stronger man than Jacob to withstand that look. Jacob knew she was playing up his role in their escape, but as he watched Runar, wondering how the deputy commissioner would react to her entreaty, he admired her scheming mind. Nikki never blinked once or even twitched a finger, merely kept her imploring gaze fixed on Runar's face.

The deputy commissioner coughed and shut his mouth with a click. He looked as if he'd swallowed a lemon; his lips formed a tight line, and his eyes narrowed dangerously. But then Runar surprised Jacob by replying in a strained voice, "If you think it's that important, then yes, the inspector will remain with you until we can get you on a flight out of here, we hope as early as tomorrow morning."

Jacob let out an inaudible breath. Runar might be displeased with him, but at least he was letting him finish out this mission, thanks to Nikki's intervention.

"Thank you," she replied, this time with a genuine smile. She didn't look at Jacob, but he could feel the relief emanating from her. "Inspector Utsi further helped me to keep hold of my most precious asset, my computer. Once I catch up on a few hours of sleep, I'd love to start working on our team's research." She sat up straighter in her chair and pointed to the backpack at her feet. "I'm not sure if you know, but I downloaded all of Tammy and Antoine's information from the cloud." As she mentioned her two colleagues' names,

Nikki paled. But she lifted her chin and went on. "I also emailed it to Dr. Morgan at the institute, so by now lots of people have access to the data. Those bastards who were out to kill me have lost," she added triumphantly.

Runar drummed his fingers on the desk. "That's good news regarding your computer, Dr. Winter." He held up a hand to forestall her when she leaned forward as if to say more. "But while data is important, those hitmen were not just after the facts and figures." Nikki's smile froze, and she sent Jacob a questioning glance.

"They're also trying to stop you from testifying at this judicial hearing," Runar said. "I believe you're considered one of the world's most renowned scientists; a specialist in your field. And after your colleague, Dr. Tammy Pittman, you would be the next most probable person in line to convey the truth to the court. A jury would listen to your testimony and be likely to believe you." Jacob could see comprehension dawning in Nikki's eyes. "Without you or Dr. Pittman to call on, it might take the prosecution team months to find a replacement to interpret your data. They'd probably have to ask for an extension to the trial. It might even cause the judge to call a mistrial. Even if they get a new hearing date, it could be years down the track before they reconvene. The fish company would be buying valuable time by getting rid of you. Could go for a lengthy period unchallenged, making millions more dollars."

"Oh, I see," Nikki said quietly. The vitality left her face as she sagged into the chair. Jacob's heart went out to her. She'd been through so much already. She honestly thought she was no longer a target. Until now, she'd remained so strong, but few normal people could deal with this kind of sustained level of fear. Not when the blows kept coming with no reprieve.

He leaned forward in his chair to catch her eye, laying a

hand on her knee, ignoring the deputy commissioner's sharp look. "You'll be fine," he soothed. "I promise I won't let anyone hurt you." When he'd first met her, he'd refused to make this kind of pledge; Tristan's death too fresh in his mind. But their enforced duration spent together had forged an unlikely bond, a bond that he couldn't ignore, and this time he was unable to keep the words from leaving his mouth.

Faan. Now he was going to have to prove to himself *and* to the deputy commissioner that he could do it right. Because he was a man of his word.

Nikki stared at him for many long seconds, her blue eyes never wavering from his face. "Good," she finally said. "Because I'm determined to stay alive." She got to her feet. "I'm determined to testify at this court case. I'm going to bring these bastards down."

The stubborn, headstrong Nikki was back. And he was extremely glad to see her. Jacob stood, turning to face his superior.

"That's good to hear," Runar said, also standing. He rounded his desk and opened the door to his office. "I give you my personal assurance, Dr. Winter, that we will get you safely on a flight to your home country. And I look forward to watching the outcome of this court case with great interest." This time it was Runar who initiated a handshake, and if Jacob wasn't mistaken, the deputy commissioner almost smiled as Nikki took his hand and shook it warmly.

"Thank you, sir."

"No problem," Runar said with an air of what could only be called joie de vivre. "It was a pleasure to meet you, Dr. Winter." He held the door and ushered her through it. "I just need a private word with the inspector; I hope that's okay?" the deputy commissioner added as Nikki turned to exit the room. When she gave a surprised nod, he continued, "If you wouldn't mind waiting in the hallway, he won't be long."

Jacob froze. Uh oh. He must've imagined that hint of a smile, because the second the door closed again, Runar's customary glare was back in place.

"I'm sure you know I'm not happy with this turn of events. The investigation into your misconduct is still ongoing. The loss of your witness was…a terrible miscalculation on your part, to say the least." Runar removed his glasses and polished a smudge off one lens before he put them on so he could study Jacob.

"I know." Jacob wanted to say more. He wanted to plead his case to the deputy commissioner. To tell him that Tristan had been the one to put himself in danger by disobeying an order to stay inside their hotel room in Malmo. The man had been whining that he needed a cigarette for hours on the drive down, but Jacob and Mårten had refused, saying it was too dangerous to stop, let alone to stand out in the open for any length of time. So, after they'd checked in to their room, Mårten had gone outside to do a quick survey of the perimeter of the hotel, and Jacob had been distracted by a phone call from the chief wanting to make sure they had arrived safely, Tristan had secretly let himself out of the room, then stood on the balcony to take his smoke. He couldn't have made a clearer target for a sniper if he'd tried. So technically it was Jacob's fault; Mårten had been outside at the time and Jacob should've been watching Tristan. If anyone was going to lose his job, it would be him.

"Well, I hope you do better with this one," the deputy commissioner replied testily. "I only put you on this case because I was desperate and you were the closest unit."

"I know," Jacob echoed, keeping a tight rein on his temper. The police deputy commissioner would not give him the chance to explain. Jacob understood he wasn't the man's favorite person, and he also knew the only reason the deputy commissioner hadn't taken the opportunity to sack him already was because Runar repected Mårten. Jacob liked to joke that Mårten was the teacher's pet, but Jacob didn't blame the deputy commissioner for his preference, because Mårten was a great cop and a decent guy all rolled into one.

Needing to change the subject, Jacob asked instead, "Will Dr. Winter be safe once she reaches American shores?"

Shooting him an aggrieved look, Runar ran a hand over his short hair and turned to sit heavily in his chair. It was the first time Jacob had seen any hint of uncertainty in the man since he'd entered the room, and his internal radar went on immediate alert. "I don't know. But it will be out of our hands. The FBI is taking this one over. They seemed incredibly keen to send a military transport to pick her up, and I believe they'll send two of their best agents to meet her plane when it lands. So…" Runar shrugged.

There was something the deputy commissioner wasn't telling him. Did he think the hitmen would follow her back to her home country? But even if they did, surely the FBI could handle it, couldn't they? The fact that they were chartering a military aircraft to come get her meant they were taking her safety seriously. So why did something feel off?

"I want to be on that plane," Jacob demanded.

"No, it's out of our jurisdiction. You can stay with her tonight, but once she's on that flight, she's no longer our problem." Jacob knew that look. The deputy commissioner had decided, and there was no way Jacob was going to change it.

But Jacob had an ace up his sleeve that he wasn't sure the deputy commissioner knew about. He held dual citizenship with both America and Sweden because he'd been born in the US. He could legally enter the United States if he wanted to. So it wasn't out of his jurisdiction, as long as he went as a civilian. But if he did that, disobeyed orders and turned rogue, then he knew he'd most likely never work as a police officer in Sweden again. He didn't know if he was prepared to make that sacrifice for a woman he barely knew. He needed more time to think. More time to assess this situation.

"Take her to the safe house on Kräftgaten. Two officers are there already, waiting for you. Get some sleep, Jacob, you look like you could use some." With that, the deputy commissioner bent his head to check his phone, dismissing Jacob.

"Yes, sir." Jacob left the room, shoulders straight and legs stiff.

When Jacob turned into the hallway, he was surprised to find it empty. Where was Nikki? She was supposed to be waiting for him right outside. Then he heard voices echoing from a few doors down, and he followed the sound. It led him to the staff lunchroom, and when he stalked through the doorway, he found Nikki seated at a table with one of the rookie cops, her hands wrapped around a mug of coffee. The pair were chatting, and both looked in his direction as he entered the room.

"Good evening, sir." The young female trainee stood at attention. "Sorry, sir, I found Dr. Winter in the hallway and thought she might be more comfortable down here."

"Yes, thank you, Aurora," Jacob replied. The girl was whip-smart, not afraid of any challenge, and she would make a great cop one day. But she was also a big pain in the ass. He wanted to growl that she could stop with the *sir*, but knew it wouldn't achieve anything. Both he and Mårten had tried on numerous occasions to get her to call them by their first names, but she insisted on using sir or inspector. Aurora had only joined the force three months ago and was still in training; was yet to be awarded an official partner. But she'd loosely attached herself to him and Mårten, begging to go out on patrol with them, or a accompany them on a case. Most of the time they refused, but that didn't seem to daunt her never-ending positivity.

He hated to admit it, but she'd done him a favor. Rather than leave Nikki loitering alone in the hallway, she'd taken her somewhere safe and out of the way. He should've thought about sending her to the lunchroom himself.

Aurora must be rostered onto the night shift, which would've started at eight p.m., but the girl looked as bright-eyed and bushy-tailed as if it was ten o'clock in the morning.

"You can sit down," he growled, indicating she should retake her seat. Sometimes her eager enthusiasm reminded him just how old and jaded he had become.

"Aurora just made me a cup of coffee," Nikki said brightly. "Would you like one too?"

"No thanks, we'd better get going," he replied, even though the aroma of freshly brewed coffee did smell enticing. "Thanks again, Aurora," he said, already turning on his heel.

"Sure thing, sir," she said, getting to her feet once more. "If there's anything else I can do to help, just let me know."

"Not tonight," he said, finding it hard to keep the weariness out of his tone now. The events of the last twenty-four hours were taking their toll.

"Thank you. It was nice to meet you, Aurora." Nikki placed her mug on the table, giving it a rueful glance as she left the room.

"You all good?" he asked once they were alone in the corridor, scrutinizing her features for signs of fatigue or fear. Of which he found both. She answered him with a weary nod, but he could tell there was something she wasn't saying. She indicated they should keep walking, and he wasn't about to argue; this wasn't the place to talk. They both needed some rest, and he needed to get away from here to somewhere he could think.

Jacob had promised to see the chief before he left, but that was now the last thing he wanted after Staff's dressing down. The chief would understand, and if he didn't, then Jacob had no energy to argue; he'd sort it out with his superior later. He'd parked Petar's Volvo in the secure underground carpark of the police headquarters, and so he led her toward the stairwell.

"Why are you up on misconduct charges?" Nikki blurted halfway down the stairs.

Jacob stopped and grasped the handrail as he whipped around to face her. "What? How do you know—"

"I was listening at the door," she replied without an ounce of remorse.

"You were what?" He could barely believe his ears. She had the audacity to listen in on a private conversation in the middle of a police department. He wasn't sure if he was proud of her or affronted.

"Well, I was until Aurora came along and found me. But I caught enough," she said. So now Jacob had another reason to thank Aurora. She must've noticed Nikki hovering too close to the door and took her out of temptation's way.

"You heard me." She put her hands on her hips, widening her already big, blue eyes at him. "What did you do wrong? I think I deserve to know."

Jacob ground his back teeth together. He'd been hoping to keep that piece of information quiet, at least until he had a verdict. But she had a point. If she was going to trust him to protect her, she needed to know whether he was capable of doing the job properly. Trouble was, he wasn't sure if he still was.

CHAPTER NINE

Nikki rolled over and punched the pillow, but it was no use, she couldn't get comfortable. She let out an agitated groan. Her body desperately needed sleep, but her mind hadn't got the memo. And staring at the ceiling for the past hour hadn't helped. Reaching for the nightstand, she flipped her phone over. Four-thirty a.m.. She sat up, her feet landing on the carpeted floor. They were still raw and inflamed, but as she eased up to standing, she could feel how much better they were already. Jacob had done a good job of treating her when they'd arrived at his hut, and she had no doubt her lower extremities might've suffered more damage if he hadn't acted so quickly.

After the whirlwind of fleeing the hitmen from Jacob's hut and then Petar's place, then their meeting with the police deputy commissioner, and learning that she was still a target, her mind refused to be calm. Now, after all that action and adrenaline, she was just supposed to stay here until her government sent someone to come and collect her? Great! She wasn't used to sitting around waiting for things to happen. She was a scientist, hard work and moving forward were the two mantras that'd got her to where she was today. She hated feeling helpless. And she also hated to depend on anyone.

She was used to solving all her own problems. But for now, her fate lay in the hands of one Swedish police officer. A very attractive, tenacious and adept police officer who carried himself with a quiet confidence. One she couldn't seem to keep out of her head.

When she'd confronted him about his misconduct charges, he'd told her everything about the failed mission in a clear, detached voice, without hesitation. How the man he was supposed to have been safeguarding had ended up with a bullet through the neck because he'd disregarded the threat and done something stupid. Jacob blamed himself for the man's death; Nikki had deduced that much, even though Jacob thought he could hide it from her by keeping his face devoid of all emotion. Because after he'd recounted what'd happened, he asked her, in that same detached voice, if she still wanted him to stay and protect her, now she knew about his incompetence on the job. She'd heard the slight catch in his voice as he said it, although he kept his gaze fixed on the wall above her head.

"Of course I do," she'd replied. It was true. She didn't doubt him for a second. Tammy may have called her stupid. May have said she was thinking with her lady parts and not with her head. And while Nikki found Jacob extremely attractive, she knew deep down that her trust was based on more than just sexual desire. There was something unfathomable about him. Call it gut instinct, but she was certain he'd put his life on the line to protect her.

Jacob was asleep in the room next door. She could feel the pull of him through the wall. That animal magnetism that was always sparking between them, even when she struggled to ignore it. It was probably the main reason for her insomnia —the fact he was lying in a bed mere meters away from where she slept—and it was doing her head in. Because her imagination was running wild, torturing her with questions, such as, did he sleep in the nude? And if he did, would all that bare, naked chest be as sculpted and muscular as she hoped?

Shit. She ran a hand through the tangles of her bed-ruffled hair. She was going to go insane if she let her mind wander like this. She didn't want to wake Jacob, but she couldn't stay here a second longer. But what was the protocol when you were sequestered in a safe-house with two police officers standing guard? Was she even allowed to leave her room?

She was about to find out. She pulled on her T-shirt and the jeans she'd thrown on back in the holiday hut—gosh, that seemed such a long time ago. One of the guards had promised someone would bring her a change of clothes in the morning, which would be nice, but for now these were all she had.

Cracking the bedroom door open, she peered out into the hallway. The two Swedish officers delegated to guard duty at the safe house had been most officious when Jacob had introduced them. Nikki had been so tired and in need of a soft bed that she'd barely registered their names. The first one had definitely been Oleg. He'd been very tall and thin, with a pointy face and pinched lips. But the second one, shorter, with dark hair and dark eyes, well, she couldn't remember his name. They'd both assured her they'd stay on watch all night and not to worry about a thing. But where were they? She didn't want them to mistake her for a hitman and shoot her where she stood. Should she call out to let them know she was awake?

Walking softly down the hallway, she peered into the main lounge room at the front of the house where a light was still on. The tall one, Oleg, sat in a high-backed winged chair reading a book.

Nikki cleared her throat, and the officer looked up, already reaching for the gun in his shoulder holster. She held up her hands, palms outward, and said, "Oh, gosh, sorry. I just wanted to grab a cup of tea or something. I can't sleep," she added lamely when Oleg continued to pierce her with his stare.

"Sure," he replied, but there was a sharp edge to his voice. "Nils is out doing a perimeter search. I'll let him know you are up."

Nils—that was the other guy's name—how could she have forgotten? She almost snorted at the man's terse reply. No compassion there, he was here to do a job, nothing more, nothing less. Nikki was also learning it was often the Swedish way, they were a serious bunch most of the time. Maybe that was a clue to why Jacob rarely smiled.

"Thanks," she replied, turning down the hallway toward where she thought the kitchen should be. Her head had been such a mess when they'd first arrived that the quick guided tour of the safe house was now a jumbled memory.

The kitchen was well-equipped, and it didn't take her long to fill the kettle and find a stash of tea and coffee supplies. Leaning her hip against the countertop, her mind wandered as she waited for the water to boil. There were so many notions swirling through her brain, she found it hard to corral just one for long enough to examine it properly.

An image of Tammy's face, alight with glee, morphed out of the millions of jumbled thoughts, striking her with an instantaneous sense of loss. The memory was from the second night of their trip they'd spent in Bodø, after being out all day collecting samples and taking observations from the research vessel in the fjord. They were all exhausted and wind-blown from their arduous day in the icy weather and had just sat down to a very welcome meal in the mess hall of the small scientific facility where they were being hosted. They were all grumbling about how cold the water was when Nikki had remembered a joke her grandmother used to tell her.

"Which is faster?" she'd asked gleefully. "Hot or cold water?" When both Tammy and Antoine had looked at her blankly, she'd replied, "Hot water. Because you can catch a cold." Nikki had laughed so hard at her own joke, remembering how it would crack her up when her grandmother told it, but it took the others a few seconds to grasp her meaning. Tammy was the first to get it, and when she did, she'd tipped her head back and roared with unrestrained laughter, snorting like a pig as she struggled to contain her mirth.

"That is the worst joke I've ever heard," she'd said through gasps of cackling. Tammy had touched her fondly on the arm, and Nikki had felt a surge of endearment at their friendly banter. She didn't have many friends, and when she found someone she could connect to, she counted each and every one dearly.

It hit her she'd never hear that wonderful snort-laugh again. Tammy was gone. Her wonderful, intelligent, witty, larger-than-life, gorgeous friend was gone. Tammy and her husband, Clark, could not have kids, and he must be absolutely devastated at her death. A wave of sadness washed over her so strong she nearly doubled over with the pain. Unexpected tears rolled down her cheeks. Part of her logical brain recognized that lack of sleep and the stress of the past twenty-four hours were catching up with her, making her more prone to letting emotions boil over. But she hadn't even had time to process the death of her good friends, and the sudden grief struck her like a ton of bricks.

In times like these, Nikki would've turned to Bradley for support. But that was before she'd caught him texting some strange woman a string of soppy endearments that he'd never once uttered to her. Bradley's exit had been swift. The moment she'd confronted him, he hadn't tried to hide it.

Instead, he'd packed his things and walked out, throwing the comment that she needed to stop being a doormat over his shoulder at her. The insult had stung, probably because she knew it was true; she found it hard to stand up for herself in a relationship and ask for what she wanted. She was always giving, but rarely taking. Bradley had destroyed what little trust she had left in men completely when he went out her door. Even though it'd been six months since she'd rid herself of that deceitful man—she was so much better off without him—she suddenly missed him terribly. Missed having someone to hold her, missed that simple human contact.

"Nikki." The softly uttered word had her swiping tears from her cheeks. Jacob was standing in the doorway.

Wearing only a pair of boxer shorts. Tight boxer shorts.

Oh, and wasn't it a sight?

"I'm fine," she said, hoping he believed her. But those dratted tears kept falling. "I'm fine," she whispered again as he stalked toward her across the kitchen.

"You're not fine." He stopped right in front of her, gaze raking her face, a deep crease marring his high forehead.

No, she guessed she wasn't.

He stepped closer, a question in those hazel eyes. Without thinking, she responded by also taking a step forward, and then his arms came around her and her cheek was against his chest. The physical contact was like a bolt of lightning to her system. Shocking, and yet exactly what she needed. It felt safe to be sheltered in his embrace. She wrapped her arms around his waist and drew in his strength, his solidity. The world around her was tilting on its axis, and Jacob seemed to be the only dependable thing she could cling to. Her traitorous body was acutely aware of how all those lean muscles of his chest were pressed up against her. This wasn't a scene from some steamy romance novel, she reminded herself; there were hitmen out to kill her, and Jacob was her protector. She should ignore the fact that his proximity lit her insides up like Bradly never had.

Tilting her head up with his thumb, Jacob stared down at her. Using that same thumb, he gently wiped away more stray tears, his touch scorching her cheeks where he traced the wet trails over her skin. Her sadness evaporated. Replaced by a feeling much more basic and fervent.

On the past two occasions when she'd stared into Jacob's eyes, she'd held back. But not this time. She wasn't sure who moved first, but he met her mouth with his own, pressed his lips onto hers and something exploded inside her. Of their own accord, her arms slipped around his neck, pulling him down. Closer, she needed him closer. His tongue brushed hers in a tangle of need.

Breaking their kiss, Jacob let his lips trail down the sensitive curve of her neck and back up again. What he was doing felt like reverence. His beard was so deliciously rough against her cheek. She tilted her head up and let out a small moan of pleasure as he whispered her name against her collarbone.

A thump from the living room made them both freeze. Then Nikki scrambled backward, her butt hitting the countertop in her hurry to get away from him. Away from what they'd just done. He also retreated, his hazel eyes that'd blazed with desire only seconds ago were now shuttered and unreadable. But the one thing he couldn't hide was the raging erection in his tight boxer shorts. At the last second, Jacob turned and opened a cupboard, as if he were searching for something, effectively putting his back to the door.

"Everything okay in here?" Oleg appeared in the doorway, a wary frown dragging his thin lips down.

"Yes," Jacob replied brusquely. "Just making Dr. Winter a cup of warm milk to help her sleep." He continued to rake through the cupboard, pushing cups and saucers around.

"No need for your assistance, Sergeant, thank you. You can go back to your post."

Nikki had to cover her mouth and pretend to cough to stifle her sudden urge to giggle like a schoolgirl. This wasn't funny; they'd just been almost sprung by the officious Oleg in the middle of a sizzling kiss. But the need to laugh nearly overtook her.

"Sure thing, sir." Oleg threw her a curious look before he turned and retraced his steps down the hallway.

"Sorry," she said, once they heard the other officer retake his seat in the lounge room, allowing her mirth to show through. She wasn't sure if she was apologizing for kissing him, or for making light of the situation.

"I'm not," he replied, throwing her a cheeky grin in return, and the heat in that grin hit her right in the solar plexus. Then his face fell, and he added, "But I should go back to my room. I don't really want to be caught like this…" He gestured to the bulge in his boxer shorts. Impressive. Even after he'd nearly been discovered in a very compromising position by a lower-ranking officer, Jacob's arousal was still clear. She must've had some kind of effect on him, she decided smugly. "As long as you're okay now," he said, taking a quick step toward her.

"Yes, I'm fine," she conceded. "I was sad about Tammy and Antoine. But you've given me something else altogether to think about."

He gave a rueful shrug and looked as if he might say more, but Oleg coughed loudly from the main room and Jacob grimaced, covered the front of his boxer shorts and disappeared down the hallway.

Wow, that was completely unexpected. She'd just discovered that the cool, in-control man she knew Jacob to be on the surface hid a secret, much more sinful side. There was a burning intensity inside Jacob Utsi, one that Nikki wanted to see more of, wanted him to unleash. On her. But this wasn't the time or the place for her salacious thoughts. She was returning to America tomorrow. He was a Swedish cop who had a job to do here. They led completely different lives on separate continents. There was no way this would work, so why was she even contemplating it?

Nikki waited until the kettle boiled, then took her hot tea back to her bedroom, walking slowly past Jacob's door. *If only…* No, there was no place for *if only* in her life right now. Her job was to survive long enough to see that Tammy and Antoine's research was used to stop that greedy Chinese corporation in its tracks. She owed them that much.

There was no chance she was going to get any more sleep in the few hours left until morning. Accepting her fate, she dragged her computer from the backpack on the floor and got into bed with it open on her lap. She may as well take advantage of this time and familiarize herself with the reams of data Tammy and Antoine had collected. Try to corral it all into some form that might make sense to her. And to a jury. From experience, she knew all her written documentation and evidence needed to be submitted to the prosecuting lawyers at least a week before the actual trial. And if she were to become the specialist up on the stand in front of the Supreme Court in Oslo, she'd better learn her stuff. But there was a lot of information to wade through. Her boss, Russell, might help her decipher the more technical material. She'd already sent him the link to all the information, but had he had an opportunity to look at any of it yet? Time to find out. She opened an email and addressed it to him, her fingers flying over the keyboard.

* * *

"You're going to do what?" Nikki wasn't sure she'd understood Jacob correctly. They were standing on the tarmac of the military air base on the outskirts of Luleå, and she had to shout to be heard. A squat, dark-gray aircraft stood ready a few hundred yards away, engines rumbling as it waited for her to board, the noise almost overwhelming. It was now mid-morning, and there was a howling wind sending ribbons of snow swirling around her ankles as she pulled her knit hat as far down as it would go. Oleg and Nils remained on guard beside the dark SUV, thirty feet or so behind Jacob, waiting for him to say his goodbyes.

"I'm coming with you on the plane. I have an American passport, so I can enter your country freely," Jacob shouted back.

Nikki was struggling to comprehend his words, and she was getting colder by the second standing out in the below zero temperatures, even though she was dressed in warm clothing and a nice thick winter jacket courtesy of the deputy commissioner, who'd had a bag of clothes delivered for her and Jacob to the safe house.

"Why?" she shouted. Why had he suddenly thrown her this curveball? All last night, after they'd been to see the deputy commissioner, she'd been telling herself that she was resigned to the fact she wouldn't be seeing Jacob anymore. She'd almost convinced herself that they'd only known each other for less than twenty-four hours and they couldn't possibly have forged a connection in that short a time. Then there was that scorching kiss in the kitchen that'd changed everything. She could've taken the next step; if she'd followed her burning desire and knocked on Jacob's door last night, she knew he would've let her in. But again, she decided there was no future for them, so she chose to put that kiss behind her and walk on past. But her stupid heart still wanted more. And here he was offering her more. At what cost, though?

"Because I made a promise that I would protect you, no matter what."

Her blood pounded hot and heavy through her veins. What she wouldn't give to explore another kiss with Jacob. To explore more than that. But, no. What she wanted was impossible. What he was about to do was impossible. He wasn't thinking logically. She had to convince him to stay.

"Yes, I realize you made me a promise. But, Jacob, this is going way beyond the scope of your duties. Way beyond anything a sane person would do. I commend your dedication, but you can't do this." A sudden thought occurred to her. "Wait. Does your boss know you're here?"

Jacob shook his head grimly.

"So you could lose your job?" Her teeth were chattering in the intense cold, and she could see Oleg and Nils becoming impatient behind Jacob. They wouldn't be able to hear what was being said, but they wouldn't be happy with the delay.

Jacob merely met her gaze, his tawny eyes giving nothing away. She could feel a sense of calm surrounding him. Could also sense his steely resolve. And she knew that nothing she could say was going to sway him from this crazy course.

"Like I said, I keep my promises." His lips turned up in a cocky half-grin that ignited the dimple in his cheek, and her chest expanded with hope, even while she let out a frustrated grunt of disapproval. This was so unbelievable; she wasn't sure if she wanted to smack that grin off his face, or reach up and kiss him till they both couldn't breathe. He was infuriating.

"You're going to do this whether or not I want you to, aren't you?"

That dimpled grin grew a little wider.

She sighed and shook her head. "Alright. But I don't reckon these air force guys will let you on the plane," she added grumpily, rubbing her gloved hands together to get some warmth into them. Jacob had warned her that her fingers and toes would still be sensitive to the cold, and he was right. Her fingers were stinging, and her feet were aching. She needed to escape this weather.

"Don't worry about that; I've got a plan." He gave her that devastating smile again, the one that made her want to run her hands through his hair and pull his mouth down to hers for another of his ravishing kisses.

Nikki couldn't wait to see Jacob try to sweet-talk his passage onto a military transport. Part of her hoped they refused him and turned his ass right back around. There was no way he should put his job on the line for her. No way in hell. But then again… Gosh, she was so confused. A large chunk of her was furious he was doing this. But a smaller, admittedly more insistent voice, was secretly happy he would be on that flight.

Jacob had raced to tell Oleg and Nils to leave without him, but Nikki wasn't waiting. She stomped toward the behemoth standing on the tarmac, heading for a set of stairs where two men in khaki stood at attention. It was bizarre to think that big airplane was here for little ol' her. And that FBI agents would be there to meet her when she landed in Seattle was also freaking her out. She guessed she had the deputy commissioner to thank for all this; he must have friends in high places. At least it meant her government was taking her situation seriously. But what would they do when they found out Jacob had accompanied her? He might regret his decision very soon.

CHAPTER TEN

Not for a single second did Jacob regret his decision to get on this flight with Nikki. As a matter of fact, he knew deep in his gut it was the right call to make. Glancing to his left, he acknowledged Nikki, who sat a few seats down from him on another one of the uncomfortable fold-down chairs set against the fuselage. She smiled but said nothing. Two official army guys were at the back of the aircraft, giving them sideways glances but leaving them to their own devices. They all wore headphones to cut out the noise, and while it wasn't freezing in here, it wasn't warm either. This military plane would usually transport large loads of cargo, or a whole regiment of personnel to be deployed to one of the many conflict zones around the world. Today, they were the only two civilians on the aircraft.

He'd had to do some fast talking to get past the soldiers, who wouldn't let him on at first. Their mission was to collect Dr. Winter and bring her back to America, they stated. There'd been no mention of a second person, and these flyboys were nothing if not sticklers for the rules. But when Jacob had produced his American passport and spun the story that he was a US citizen who might also be in danger from the squad of hitmen—keeping his true identity as a

Swedish cop under wraps—they'd had to take another look at him. All the while, Nikki had been glaring down at him from the doorway into the plane, not saying a word, but making it clear with her arctic-blue stare she was not happy.

Jacob had thanked the powers that be that'd allowed him to hold dual citizenship. And he also thanked his mother for urging him to keep both passports updated, telling him that while his heart was Sámi, he may never know when he'd need to take a trip to his country of birth. Not to see his father; that was never on the table. His father had disowned both him and Rikka the day they left American shores, and they'd had no contact since.

Jacob's dad was a dick, no two ways about it. Jacob didn't miss him at all, and had no urge to reconnect with him. Not now, not ever. He'd bonded more with both of his uncles after he'd returned to Sweden than he ever had with his biological dad. Sometimes he wondered what his mother had seen in him in the first place. But he'd never been brave enough to ask that question, and he knew that love did strange things to a person's heart and mind, altering reason and logic until it was often too late.

He risked another glance at Nikki and tried not to think about love or acting stupidly in the face of infatuation.

He also had Mårten to thank for being here. Without Mårten having brought his passport to him early this morning, he wouldn't be on this flight. Mårten had returned from leave to come home to Luleå late last night when he'd heard about Jacob's high-stakes mission, in case he could be of any help. That was just like Mårten, always dependable, always having Jacob's back.

"Rydberg sent me a message, and so I hightailed at home," Mårten had said over the phone when Jacob had called him once they'd reached the safe house earlier this morning. All he'd really wanted was his partner's advice, expecting his call to wake a sleepy Mårten, who should still be in Stockholm. But he was more than delighted to hear he'd just arrived back in town and was wide-awake and eager to help. "So, what's your take on all this?" Mårten had cut straight to the chase. Rydberg would've already given him the official line, but Mårten knew there would be much more to it than that.

"I know you hate to use the term *gut instinct,*" Jacob grimaced at the phone, imagining Mårten's face when he said those words; his partner detested that phrase. "But I have this feeling. I need to see this through to the end. I want to get on that plane with her tomorrow." If anyone understood, it would be Mårten. He wouldn't question why; he would just ask what he could do to help. Which is exactly what he did.

"Can you bring my American passport for me? I can tell you where to find it in my house." Mårten had a key to Jacob's house, as did he for Mårten's; they trusted each other implicitly.

"Of course," Mårten had replied, but Jacob heard the note of caution in his tone. After a moment's hesitation, Mårten added, "She must be pretty special."

Jacob didn't reply. He couldn't completely understand it all himself, let alone convey his convoluted feelings about this case and about Nikki to his best mate and partner. All he could do was hope that Mårten read between the lines.

Mårten gave a deep sigh. "I'll do my best to head off Rydberg for as long as I can. But the rest is up to you. Look for me in the early morning. I'll message you when I'm close," he added before hanging up.

Mårten had come through, handing over the passport as Jacob stood in the doorway, Nils watching their meet-up from his station at the front gate, but not interfering. Jacob had told the other two officers his partner was dropping off some essential documents, and neither of them had argued. He was sure word of this would reach Rydberg eventually. Then

Mårten would be in nearly as much shit as Jacob.

Mårten had thumped Jacob on the back in a manly version of a hug right before he left, catching Jacob off guard. "You take care," Mårten had said, then hightailed it out through the front gate. Neither of them was the touchy-feely type, and Mårten's uncharacteristic show of sentiment left Jacob with a strange lump in his throat. In that moment, he realized he was possibly closer to Mårten than he was to his own sister; Mårten was like a brother to him. He would miss him if he ever left the force.

The flight had been long and arduous, over eleven hours in the air, and Jacob had plenty of time to dissect how many types of stupid he was being, and just how much trouble he was getting himself and Mårten into. But it soon became clear from the activity of the two army officers in the cargo hold and the drop in pressure inside the aircraft that they were on their descent into Seattle. Both he and Nikki had caught a few hours of sleep, lying down along the row of crash seats. Not the most comfortable of beds, but he'd had worse.

Jacob unbuckled his belt and moved to the seat next to Nikki. They'd hardly spoken during the flight; he could see in her eyes she was still mad at him. Maybe mad wasn't the word, more like frustrated or exasperated. But he was a big boy; he knew what he was doing. Knew what was at stake here. And something about Runar's veiled warning had got to him. Call it a hunch, but he just wanted to make sure Nikki was safe. To finish the mission he'd started. Once he'd seen her delivered to her front door, and confirmed her protection detail were up to scratch, he'd hightail it back home. Although why he thought he could do a better job than the FBI was anyone's guess.

He took her hand in his, and she let him, which told him she was more nervous than she'd admit. Her hand was small and cool in his own. Her other hand rested possessively on top of her backpack, which was shoved under her seat. They sat, unspeaking but still connected, until the plane touched down.

Two FBI agents, a man and a woman, were waiting at the bottom of the steps as they exited the aircraft, just as Nikki had been promised. Dressed in civilian clothing, their upright stance and sharp, wary glances gave them away. Because of the different time zones, it was still the middle of the day here in Seattle, and a bright sun shone out of a brittle blue sky, almost blinding him as he walked down the stairway behind Nikki. It was cold, but not bone-crunchingly freezing like it had been in Luleå. Thanks to Runar, Jacob had at least been able to discard his white snowsuit for the fresh jeans and jumper the deputy commissioner had sent over. But Jacob also welcomed the warm jacket Runar had included, because that Seattle wind had an icy edge to it.

"I'm Agent Sabitino, and this is Agent Miller," the male agent said brusquely. They both flashed their badges, and he held out his hand to greet Nikki and then Jacob. They didn't look in the least surprised to see Jacob, and he assumed word of his sudden addition to the flight had already reached their ears.

"Thanks so much," Nikki said on a gust of outward breath. "You don't know how good it is to hear an American accent again," she added. "And how wonderful it is to be on home soil. After… Well, I'm assuming you are aware of what happened in Sweden?" she asked.

They both nodded, stone-faced, giving nothing away. Something niggled low down in Jacob's gut.

"We'll be taking care of you now," Sabitino said, but his gaze never met Nikki's, his eyes roving across the deserted tarmac instead.

"Come with us, Dr. Winter. We'll take you home. I'm sure you'll be wanting a hot shower and the comfort of your own bed," Agent Miller added, but there was no softness, her face never showing the hint of a smile. "And you, Mr. Utsi, of course." The woman gestured for both of them to precede her.

"Oh, good, you're taking me to my house. I was worried I'd have to go into another safe house or something," Nikki chatted happily with the female agent.

Jacob heard her reply that it wasn't warranted in these circumstances, and that at least four FBI agents would stand guard outside day and night until either the trial had run its course, or they caught the hitmen. But he was only half-listening. Something wasn't quite right, but he couldn't figure out exactly what it was. He should be pleased that the American government was addressing Nikki and her predicament seriously. They clearly had a vested interest in protecting her. Making sure she stayed alive to testify at this corporate court case. Why weren't they taking her to a safe house, though? If they were having to invest the manpower to watch over her house, it would make more sense to do it where they could control everything. Jacob was sure they had their reasons, but he still worried at the thought like it was a sore tooth, all the while watching the male agent warily out of the corner of his eye, trying to decide if he could take him down if it came to a hand-to-hand fight. Probably. The guy was about Jacob's height and weight, but Jacob would have surprise on his side. No one knew he was a trained police officer with many tools in his street fighting combat arsenal.

The agents led them to a large, black limousine and ushered them into the back seat, where yet another man sat waiting for them. Nikki slid in beside him, still chatting easily to Miller, who took a seat across from her. Jacob hurried into the car, sitting next to Miller.

Miller identified the other man in the back of the limousine as Agent Linstead, while Sabitino got into the front passenger seat. Linstead greeted Nikki with a smile, more animated than his two associates, nodding in greeting to Jacob, and shaking his hand earnestly. They were never introduced to the driver, even when Jacob cast him a curious glance. The guy was obviously another agent, with that dead-eyed stare and quiet, menacing aura surrounding him.

The half-hour trip to Nikki's house was uneventful, and Nikki gave a small clap of glee as they drove into her driveway, happy to be home. Jacob glimpsed a cute cottage, painted dove-gray, with white trim, and a white picket fence enclosing the front garden. It was what he would've imagined Nikki living in. Cozy and inviting with a boho vibe.

Agent Sabitino came around from the front seat and opened the door, signaling for Jacob to exit first. Which he did, but then suddenly he found Sabitino crowding him, not allowing him to step away from the vehicle, not letting Jacob continue up the driveway. Which was understandable, maybe they needed to search the house once more to make sure it was safe before they let them in. So Jacob stood with his back to the car, watching Sabitino with one eye while he extended a hand to help Nikki alight.

It wasn't until she tried to exit the vehicle and Agent Sabitino stepped in front of her, also blocking her path, that those small niggling doubts Jacob had been trying to ignore jangled loudly. He gripped her hand tighter and clenched his other hand into a fist, readying himself. Ready for what, he wasn't sure. Unexpectedly, Agent Miller materialized beside Sabitino; she must've quietly exited the other side and moved around the rear of the vehicle more swiftly than Jacob could've imagined.

"Oh, just one more thing. Before you go in, we'd like you to hand over your computer and your phone, if you don't mind, Dr. Winter," Agent Linstead said from behind Nikki. "You too, Mr. Utsi," he added smoothly.

Faan. He should've expected something like this. Although what he could've done about it was anybody's guess. There were four of them, and only one of him.

"What do you mean?" Nikki stopped, one foot on the driveway and one foot still in the car, her backpack slung over one shoulder, a confused look clouding her face. "I need my computer so I can work on the case. It's—"

Jacob pulled her all the way out of the car and then pushed her behind him, so she was jammed up against the vehicle and partly shielded by his body, interrupting whatever else she'd been about to say. These guys weren't about to bargain with her. They were dead serious. Jacob just wished he could figure out what was going on. Were they real FBI agents? They looked the part. He berated himself for not having checked their ID badges more thoroughly. Or were they more hitmen hired by the Chinese fish company to do their dirty work on American soil? It seemed unlikely; these individuals all appeared highly trained and professional, but it couldn't be discounted.

"What the fuck is going on?" he growled, locking his gaze on Sabitino. The agent stared back, not flinching, and Jacob saw something dark flash through the other man's eyes. He was dangerous. The sort of man who didn't shy away from using force when necessary—even when it wasn't necessary. Jacob knew men like Sabitino, who liked the job because it allowed them to unleash the veiled violence they kept hidden just below the surface. Miller stood beside Sabitino, her face just as hard as her colleague's, but there was no sign of the suppressed brutality in her. A more level-headed agent, she wouldn't harm them, but she also wasn't going to let them get away.

"Nothing is going on." Linstead's voice drifted out of the car door. Funny, Jacob hadn't picked him as the leader of the pack, but he was making his status crystal clear now. He wished he could see Linstead's face, try to work out what was going on in his head. "All you need to do is comply with our request, and then you can proceed safely into your house." His tone was mild, but Jacob could hear the veiled malice in it. The driver had turned in his seat, watching the proceedings with interest, and Jacob knew he was primed to leap out of the vehicle and help Sabitino and Miller if required.

"But why do you want my computer and my phone?" Nikki asked again, struggling to keep up. Jacob pressed her harder against the car, wishing that she'd stay quiet. If things got violent, he wanted all their attention on him. And away from her. And that would not happen if she kept challenging them. Especially Sabitino, who was looking for an excuse to get rough. Jacob had been in plenty of hairy situations before. There were times for action, and then there were times for diplomacy. And possibly even capitulation, especially if it meant you lived to fight another day. This was definitely one of those times. There was no way he'd be able to defeat or outrun four trained operatives. Not with Nikki to look after as well. She needed to comply, then they'd be allowed into the house unmolested as Linstead had promised, where they could regroup and figure out what was going on.

"To keep them safe. Just like we're going to protect you," Linstead replied.

"Why are you doing this? Are you even real FBI agents?" Nikki spat, pushing against Jacob, trying to get to Sabitino. He could feel her practically vibrating with anger behind him. Even though he was heavier than she was, he had to use all his strength to hold her back. He could just imagine her marching right up to the glowering agent, hands on hips and flinging daggers from her eyes straight to Sabitino's heart as she confronted him. *Fann*, why did she have to be so stubborn? Part of him admired her guts, standing up to four specially trained agents. But she didn't know what she was getting herself into, and he needed to stop this before someone got hurt.

"Yes, we are, ma'am," Sabitino replied tersely. "And we're following orders. So hand over your hardware. Please," he added, as an afterthought.

Why were they confiscating the computer and phones? It made no sense. Did they want to inspect them for malware? Or hidden bugs? But if that were the case, couldn't they just send a tech guy to the house? And by taking their cells, the FBI were stopping them from communicating with the outside world. That warning voice got louder, and he broke out in a cold sweat as understanding flooded through him. That was exactly what the FBI wanted. To cut them off. But why? Sabitino took a menacing step toward Jacob, and he knew he was running out of time. He could figure out their motives later; right now, he needed to get Nikki to safety.

"Nikki, stop," Jacob growled out of the corner of his mouth. Simultaneously, he dug in his front pocket and handed over his phone, which Miller took from his outstretched hand with a grim smile. "Give them your bag," Jacob added, when he could feel her still hesitating.

"Your friend has the right idea," Linstead said from inside the car, and Jacob noticed a small smirk alighting on Sabitino's lips. The guy was anticipating having to seize the bag from Nikki using force, and he liked the idea.

"Now, Nikki. Please do as they ask," Jacob implored. He dared not take his eyes off Sabitino to turn his head to look at her, but he hoped she heard the truth in his voice. She needed to do this. She sagged against his back, some of the tension draining out of her body, and he let out a small huff of relief.

"Fine. But I'm going to be talking to your superiors about this," she snapped. She wriggled behind him, and he took a step forward to allow her to remove the backpack from her shoulder. She handed it over with a sullen pout, her pretty face a mask of fury. "If your boss wants me to testify at this court case, then I need my computer back as soon as possible."

"Thank you, Dr. Winter." It was Miller who spoke, shooting Sabitino an undecipherable look when he snatched the bag from Nikki's hand. "And your cell as well, please." She held out a hand and waited while Nikki grimaced, then finally dug in her jacket pocket and handed over her phone.

"Don't *'thank you, Dr. Winter'* me," she snapped. "I don't know what the FBI is playing at, but this is not helping. Are you even going to let me testify?" No one moved, but the stupid smirk on Sabitino's face got a little wider, giving Nikki her answer. She turned on her heel and pushed between the two agents, marching up her driveway toward her house. Jacob hurried after her, leaving the operatives to bring up the rear, but only after they handed Nikki's backpack and both phones in to Linstead. Without even glancing back, Nikki bent down and retrieved a spare key from underneath a pot plant and had the front door open just as the two agents made it up the small set of stairs and onto the front porch. Jacob followed her inside and was right behind her shoulder as she turned to face the FBI agents.

"Like we said," Sabitino started. "We'll have four agents guarding your house. Two out front, and two out back to make sure you are safeguarded. So if you need anything—"

She slammed the door in Sabitino's face. "Yeah, right," she shouted. "You're not safeguarding us. You're keeping us prisoner." Then she kicked the wooden paneling and pivoted sharply, running straight into his chest. His arms came up around her instinctively. He wasn't sure if it was more for protection or for comfort. She was small and slight in his arms, but as tightly tensed as a bowstring. She drew back a little so she could look up into his face. "Am I wrong?" she asked.

For a millisecond, he thought about denying it. Telling her she wasn't now a prisoner in her own home. But she deserved the truth.

"No." He brushed a lock of blonde hair away from her face. "I'm not sure what's going on, but they don't want us leaving here. And they don't want us to contact anyone outside, either."

Her eyes clouded with angry tears. "Why? Why don't they want me testifying?"

He didn't know why. And he wasn't completely sure what was happening here. They might still let her attend the court case. Their non-answers had been evasive, but not conclusive. He had a few ideas about why they would try to control her access to things like computers and phones, but none of them were good, and so he didn't air them in front of Nikki. Not until he got more of a grasp on what was going on. His hand moved from her face down her shoulder, then slipped around her narrow waist, drawing her in closer. She felt so good in his arms. Even with two agents standing guard on the other side of the door only a few feet away, he couldn't ignore the way her body molded to his; every one of her curves seemed to fit into all his hard edges perfectly.

"It could be temporary," he hedged, not fully concentrating on what he was saying anymore. The feel of her thighs pressed against his was sending tingling shocks of electricity through him. He tried to focus on their conversation. "They might just be checking that everything is legit. Then they'll return our items…"

"You don't really believe that, do you?"

He shook his head. Something about the sly look on Sabitino's face, and the smooth calmness of Linstead's assurance both screamed deceit to Jacob. If only he could contact Mårten. His levelheaded partner would have this figured out in no time. And even if he couldn't, he'd know who to call to help them out of this pickle.

The tears in Nikki's eyes glistened but didn't fall as she drew in a fortifying breath. "Oh, well, we'll just have to find a way out of this." She stood a little straighter, the movement pushing her pert breasts harder into his ribcage; he could feel them even through the layers of their winter jackets. His cock responded immediately. Did she realize what she was doing to him? He should step away, end this before it went any farther.

"I've got a landline. Could we use that?" she asked hopefully, widening those big, blue eyes at him. The urge to kiss her was just about unstoppable.

Jacob shook his head. "If it's even working, they'll have tapped it for sure," he murmured. The place was probably bugged as well, but he didn't tell her, not wanting her to freak out. But that thought slipped from his mind almost instantaneously when she tilted her head to the side and her face softened as if realizing how close his mouth was to hers. Her tongue darted out to wet her lips, and he stared, fascinated, at their slick, cherry-pink plumpness. He'd already tasted that sweetness, but now he wanted more. He couldn't remember lowering his head, all he knew was that the allure of her mouth was drawing him in.

Oleg had interrupted their last kiss before they'd even had a chance to explore each other. But their chemistry had been undeniable. And now they were alone in her house, with nothing and no one to interfere. His mouth crushed down on hers, letting her know how much he wanted her, not withholding anything this time.

She moaned and tipped her head back, allowing him full access to those delicious lips. Without breaking their kiss, she drew down the zipper of his jacket, and slipped her hands inside, underneath the layers of jumper and T-shirt to feather

her fingers up over his lower abs then around his ribs to knead the muscles on each side of his spine. His skin pebbled at her touch, wanting more.

"My bedroom is the first door on the right," she said, pulling her mouth from his, voice ragged.

"I'm not sure…" He could barely speak; the sensual pull of her eyes, her lips, her swaying hips beneath his hands was almost too much to bear. But someone needed to be the sensible one here. There were a million reasons they shouldn't do this. The first being the four FBI agents standing guard outside.

Her pupils dark with desire, she whispered, "I need this, Jacob. More than anything right now."

Did he do this? Did he drop all pretense of protocol and professionalism and follow his cravings?

She took him by the hand and led him down the darkened hallway. And he gave no resistance; he followed willingly behind. At least it was warm in here; Nikki must've left the heat on while she was away. Or else the FBI had turned it on while they'd been searching the house. Because he had no doubt the agents had been in here to make sure there was no way for them to escape, and no other way for them to contact the outside world.

When she closed the bedroom door, she dropped his hand and tugged impatiently at her clothing as if in a fervor to rid herself of all encumbrances. He was so fascinated watching this amazing woman reveal herself as she stripped off her jacket and jumper, then boots and jeans, he dared not move. Until she finally stood naked in front of him. His mouth went dry at the sight of her. Nothing in this world was more beautiful than Nikki Winter. Skin pale and smooth in the sliver of light leaking in around the drawn curtains. Long hair left to fall over slim shoulders unimpeded. She was magnificent.

"Do you need some help?" she enquired, quirking one eyebrow up as he continued to stare, mesmerized.

Galvanized into action, he began shedding his clothing just as rapidly as she had. But his efforts were seemingly not fast enough for her liking, because she came to him and undid his belt, her nimble fingers unfastening his buttons, and pushing his jeans over his hips. Then he was naked too, her hands running all over his body. Exploring, appreciating. Her touch heated his skin everywhere her fingertips landed until he could take no more.

Picking her up in his arms as if she were as light as a feather, he carried her over to the large bed in the middle of the room. The rest of her bedroom remained a mystery to him as he focused on her and only her.

CHAPTER ELEVEN

A small part of Nikki couldn't believe she was about to do this. To make love to Jacob. But like she'd told him in the hallway. She needed this. She wanted this. The past few days had been a nightmarish whirlwind. With only one constant. Jacob. Sexy as hell, badass cop Jacob, who protected her when no one else could. There were so many reasons she shouldn't sleep with him, but she'd banished all objections from her mind and her heart for now. This might be their sole chance to be together, and she would not regret choosing him, even if it were only for this single perfect moment in time. This was just sex, she reminded herself. A way to release all the stress and fear and anxiety of the last several days. A way to celebrate life.

Jacob's naked body lay heavy over hers, and she wriggled against him, savoring all his hot skin pressed against hers. He was devouring her mouth with his, and she let her head fall back against the pillow, pulling him down to follow her. His lips eventually left hers, but only to kiss her face, sink his tongue into the dip at the base of her throat, taste her.

Soon, his mouth was doing wicked things to her breasts and then her belly, then even lower down, and she lost awareness of anything that wasn't Jacob. The intensity within built until she was whimpering for him to give her release.

"Condom. Second drawer on the right," she panted, pointing in the direction of her nightstand. She didn't know if he carried protection, but she wasn't taking any chances, not even when she was this desperate to have him inside her. She watched him roll on the condom, and she lay back and beckoned to him. He lowered down, hovering over her body, biceps bulging as he held himself a few centimeters above, asking the question with his eyes.

"Yes," she whispered her needy response. Oh, yes. This was everything she'd wanted and more, and so she arched her back, her hips colliding with his, pushing her core against his erection. He was so hot and hard for her, and she was so ready for him. Tantalizingly slowly, Jacob eased his cock between her legs, and she opened for him, like a flower to the sun. Until, in a rush of heat and sensation, he was inside her. Oh, the feeling was incomparable, nothing else on earth felt this good.

Together they moved in the slow rhythm of sensual pleasure until she knew she was close. Oh, so close. "Jacob," she pleaded. "Jacob." His name became a mantra on her lips, then soon turned to a moan as she could hold back no longer and tumbled over the edge, her climax fast and shockingly intense. She heard him utter a groan of his own, and then he shuddered and took his own satisfaction.

They lay entangled in each other's arms for moments uncounted, her breathing becoming normal again, their skin slick with sweat where they were joined.

At last Jacob rolled off her, disposing of the condom, then lifting the blankets so they could both crawl underneath. She'd left the heating on low while she'd been away, so she didn't have to come home to a freezing house, and while she hadn't noticed the coolness of the air when they'd been making love, her skin welcomed the coziness of flannel sheets now.

They lay facing each other, not speaking, content to be cocooned in each other's arms. Nikki admired the strong planes of Jacob's cheekbones, his slightly crooked nose as she stared into his amazing hazel eyes. Jacob's eyelids fluttered closed, even though he valiantly tried to keep them open. She didn't blame him; it'd been a long few days and neither of them had slept much. Lethargy made her limbs heavy, but her brain was still too wired to shut her eyes just yet. Which left her an opportunity to study Jacob as he lay sleeping and try to untangle all the knots in her mind as to how she felt about him.

The sex had been amazing. And she'd discovered a lot about Jacob today in her bed. Over the time Nikki had known Jacob, he'd come across as calm and competent, radiating a don't-fuck-with-me vibe. The man was intimidating. Even when he'd been outnumbered this morning in the driveway, she'd felt the brutality that Jacob kept hidden just below the surface ready to be unleashed; he'd been prepared to fight to the death with those agents if he'd had to. But now she had a unique insight; in bed she'd seen another side of Jacob. A tender side, vulnerable even. He was an attentive lover, compassionate and giving. She almost felt as if she were being worshiped as he'd stroked the skin over her hipbone, and kissed her collarbone so gently, intent on driving her slowly insane. He was far more committed to her pleasure than Bradley had ever been.

That notion stopped her in her tracks. Bradley had been nowhere in her thoughts while they'd made love, which surprised her. It was now a little over six months since she'd found out about Bradley's cheating and ended their relationship. Half a year since she'd made love with a man. And while she'd missed the sheer physical indulgence of the carnal act, her heart had been too wounded to want to move on. Until now. One touch from Jacob and she'd lit up like a Christmas tree, zinging with awareness and want. She couldn't remember having this kind of intense attraction to any other man.

But what did that mean? For her? And for Jacob? Was there any kind of future for them? Or was this the beginning and the end all rolled into one? She was a scientist who lived in Seattle. He was a police officer who lived in Sweden. It didn't seem like there was any way they could make this work, even if they wanted to. Which she wasn't sure she did.

She and Bradley had been together for three years. Had been in love, or so she thought. There'd been no actual discussion about getting married and having kids, but she'd always assumed it was on the cards at some stage in the future. That one day Bradley would get down on one knee and produce a ring. And then after he'd betrayed her so horribly, she was no longer sure where she stood on the matter of marriage, or even another relationship. She'd actively steered away from men, not wanting to put her heart out there again so soon. If ever.

Then Jacob had barged into her sauna and into her life.

Gosh, she didn't know if he actually was single? The conversation had never come up, and today they'd been so caught up in the swift intensity, the idea he might have a partner hadn't even occurred to her. She was pretty sure he was a man of principles, and wouldn't cheat on a lover, girlfriend, or wife. He wore no ring on his finger, but a lot of men didn't. That would be one of the first questions she was going to ask when he woke up.

The lethargy in her muscles was finally taking over her brain, and her eyelids became heavy. Time for all those uncertainties later. They were stuck in her house for the foreseeable future with nowhere to go and nobody they could contact. There was nothing they could do while the FBI stood guard right outside her door. So, she may as well follow Jacob's example and get some much-needed sleep. Maybe things would become clearer when they woke up.

* * *

Nikki moved sluggishly around the kitchen, covering an enormous yawn as she turned on the coffee machine. She and Jacob had slept like the dead for six hours straight, neither of them moving out of their lover's embrace. Now it was evening, and she stared out the window at the bleak, wintry skies trying to rouse herself from her daytime snooze. There was no sign of the FBI agents who were supposed to be guarding the house on her front porch, but she had no doubt they were there somewhere. Which was a good thing, because if she spied one of them, she was likely to go out and give them a piece of her mind.

She knew part of her listlessness was due to jet lag. But more of it was the hopelessness she was now feeling. She'd arrived back in America full of determination to use the data from her research to bring down the greedy Chinese company. But that plan had been put in limbo, and she was at a loss as to what to do next.

There was a knock at the door, and Nikki jumped, wondering if those pesky agents could read her mind. She knew she looked a sight, her hair all in tangles and wearing sweats, which she'd hastily pulled on as an afterthought when she remembered there were strangers watching from outside. She was of two minds whether to answer the door. But when she looked out through the peephole, the brown paper bag being held up by Miller convinced her to open it.

"We thought you might need some supplies," Miller said, but Nikki was still too angry for olive branches, and she snatched the bag with a haughty sniff then slammed the door closed in the other woman's face. She was being petty, but the satisfaction was nonetheless immense. There was bread, butter, fresh fruit, milk and other staples in the bag, which was good, because Nikki had left the fridge practically empty.

Jacob emerged from the bedroom wearing only a T and his jeans at the sound of the door slamming. He came up behind her as she put the bag on the kitchen countertop and pulled her around gently into a hug, kissing the top of her head as she lay it against his chest.

"Hey, babe." Her heart kicked hard in her ribcage at his easy endearment. No one else had ever called her babe. It felt…right somehow. She circled her arms around his waist, and they stood for many moments in their quiet embrace as she absorbed the heat of him, desperately needing his strength. "Are you okay?" he asked at last, and she lifted her face and kissed him fiercely, crushing her body against his, telling him without words how okay she was. There were no regrets, no recriminations, only a feeling of calm and of being blessed. What they'd just done had been wonderful. Even if the rest of her life had gone to shit, this was one bright, shining moment she'd remember forever.

"I'm fantastic," she replied. "You?"

"Is there a word for better than fantastic?" He murmured against her hair. "Because if there is, then that's what I am."

She sought his lips again, luxuriating in the simple feel of being thoroughly kissed. As their kiss deepened, a surge of heat rolled through her, pooling low in her belly, and she ground her hips against his, wrapping one leg around his thigh and batting her eyelids at him.

"We could go back to bed," she suggested, tracing a finger down the side of his chiseled face, loving the way his pupils dilated as he stared back, hazel eyes going dark and dangerous.

"We could," he replied, letting his mouth trail the length of her neck. But a loud rumble from his stomach shattered the moment, and she laughed, breaking their embrace.

"Maybe we should have something to eat first. To get our strength back," she said with a sigh. Thinking about it, she was famished as well. They hadn't eaten since a quick breakfast at the safe house in Luleå, and that was over twenty hours ago. The coffee maker was already filling the kitchen with the familiar smell of her morning brew, so she put four pieces of bread in the toaster. Even though it was dinner time, her internal clock was confused, and a simple meal was all she could manage right now.

Jacob went around to the other side of the table and took a seat, staring out the window into the front yard, a pensive frown on his brow. Nikki leaned against the countertop and indulged herself for a moment, delighting in the rumpled, half-asleep version of him. His back and shoulder muscles flexed beneath his shirt as he moved to rest his chin in the palm of his hand; muscles she could now recount every firm ridge and solid plane in detail. Muscles that she'd had the ultimate indulgence of running her fingers over only a few hours ago. And could do so again if she so wished. The idea was intoxicating.

She no longer saw him solely as the hardened, always-in-control cop who'd saved her life back in the snow. Now she knew his body intimately. Knew what was between his thighs and the immense pleasure it brought. Knew he had a gentle side that he never showed to the rest of the world. Her perception of Jacob was forever changed. For the past few days he'd been her savior, her protector, her shield. But now he was so much more. He was a lover, a confidante. A combustible connection had formed between them, driven by passion and deep emotion. But she wasn't sure how to process all that. Wasn't sure what it meant.

It'd all been shaped by the understanding that it might never happen again. The intensity had been real at the time, but what about now, in the cold light of day? Was she falling in love with Jacob? No, it wasn't realistic; they'd only known each other for two days. Yes, they'd built an unshakeable bond, forged by forced proximity and dire circumstances, but that was all. It was ridiculous even to be thinking about the L word. Her mind swirled with all the knotted complexity of everything they'd just shared, but she was incapable of processing it all right now. Whatever this was that they were doing, love just wasn't possible. Perhaps if things had been different…

The toast popped with a loud bang, startling them both, and breaking her twisted thoughts. Gosh, what had she been doing? This was no time to be wallowing in *ifs and maybes*; first and foremost, they needed to get out of this predicament. She could think about matters such as love and relationships later.

"I can only offer you strawberry jam," she said, hoping her voice sounded normal as she reached for the toast.

"That'd be great," he replied, getting up from the table and taking the two mugs she'd laid out on the bench to the coffeepot to fill them. Once they had their toast and coffee, they each took a seat, and there was silence for long moments as they took great bites of their food.

"Best toast I've ever tasted," Jacob quipped.

"That's because it's post-coital toast. And everyone knows post-coital toast is the best," she quipped back.

They smiled stupidly at each other, and Nikki felt something expand in her chest. Why did this feel so easy? So right? It wasn't fair. She wanted to have the time and space to explore whatever was happening between them. But the world had conspired against them, and she needed to remind herself that Jacob wasn't for her. Once this was over—whenever that might be—Jacob would return to Sweden. And she'd be left here alone. That thought hit Nikki like a bucket of cold water, and the smile fell from her face as she turned toward her meal, which now didn't seem so appealing.

Time to come back to reality. They needed to talk about what was going to happen next. How they might get out of this situation, if that were even possible.

"I thought they were saving me by bringing me home," she said, staring down at her plate. "They might've saved me from being shot by a bunch of hitmen, but that's about all. Now it seems they're keeping me—us—prisoners. But to what end?" She lifted her eyes and met his. "Someone doesn't want me to testify in that court case, do they?"

"That's the impression I'm getting," he said, his gaze darting around the room.

"But who? And why? I mean, your deputy commissioner told me *the government* organized my military flight home, but I didn't even think to ask what that actually meant. Are we talking about one particular agency here? Or one particular person? Someone high up, perhaps in the Senate or even Congress? And what does that *someone* hope to achieve if Diàoyú Aquaculture gets to keep its fish farming licenses?" Her mind refused to make sense of it all; there were too many permutations.

"I don't know." But as Jacob said the words, he put his finger to his lips, then pointed at the walls.

What the…?

"Oh." Nikki drew back in horror as she suddenly realized what he was implying. The FBI might have bugged her house. They were listening in on everything they said. Was it possible? Oh, God, had they been listening as she and Jacob had made love? The idea made her so angry she couldn't sit on her stool any longer, and she got up to stamp around the kitchen.

But Jacob grabbed her arm and steered her toward the hallway. "I think it's time for a shower, don't you?"

What was he doing? Had he gone mad? Now wasn't the

moment for getting clean. As Jacob guided them both into the small bathroom and shut the door behind them, Nikki was seething with both the audacity of the FBI and confusion as to what the hell he thought he was doing. But when Jacob turned the sink faucet on full and then reached in and activated the shower as well, her confusion vanished in a flash of insight.

"They can't hear us over the sound of the water?" she asked in a half-whisper.

"I hope not," Jacob replied, perching on the side of the bathtub and patting a spot next to him, indicating she should sit. "But try to keep your voice down," he added with a grimace. "It depends on what tech they're using, and if they have video and audio."

Nikki's head sprang up. Did she now have to be worried that the FBI might have video footage of her and Jacob in bed together? The grinding rage that'd been building in her gut turned to white-hot fury. How dare they? It made her more determined than ever to get out of here and somehow make it to that courtroom in Norway. If she could only testify, then she could spit in the face of those double-crossing agents.

She asked the question that was now burning brightly in her mind. "Is this still related to Diàoyú? Are they really FBI agents? Or are they some kind of Chinese deepfake decoy?" Could the company's influence reach that far onto American soil? It was bloody scary if that were true.

"I wondered the same thing for a while too," Jacob admitted. "I'm not a hundred percent sure, but I think that'd be hard to forge. They certainly looked and felt like the real thing. Although who they're working for is another matter completely." He cocked his head to the side and ran a hand through his hair as she watched his reflection in the mirror above the sink. His brow wrinkled with the intensity of his contemplation.

Nikki trusted his judgment about the agents being genuine. As a highly trained professional, she was pretty sure he'd be able to recognize the same qualities in another agent or officer. But what was he saying? Was there corruption within the FBI? And if so, where did the corruption stem from? The team leader, the entire team, or an individual further up the chain directing the unit?

"So, do you think this mission to keep me from testifying is being driven directly by someone in the FBI?"

"I can't be sure," Jacob admitted. "But I can't see what they would gain from any of this. The FBI is just a tool for the government. They're supposed to handle federal issues and protect national security, so I'm uncertain why they would want to interfere in an international court case, unless this has something to do with a transnational crime, or criminal gang. And while they run plenty of intelligence-gathering operations both inside and outside of the US, they're most often connected with counter-terrorism, and I can't see that a Chinese-run fish farm in Norway could be associated with violent extremism. Can you?"

"Not really." Unless there was something they were missing, this was more about corporate greed than any sort of terrorism. Which brought them back to the same question. "What is to be gained by the US government—or perhaps even a single entity within that government—if this court case doesn't go through?" she asked thoughtfully. "And how could this all be linked to Diàoyú?"

"Hmm," Jacob mused. "Someone with influence over the FBI is using them to achieve a certain agenda; that much is for sure. Is there a corrupt government official on the inside driving this, or is an outside entity putting pressure on someone internally? Like a high-up Chinese official, for instance," he said, running a hand over his perplexed brow. "One thing is for sure, when this much money is at stake, people will do just about anything."

Which brought them back to square one? They had absolutely no idea why anyone would want to stop her from attending the court case. Back in Sweden, they'd been pretty sure the men trying to kill her were hired by Diàoyú. But now that she was back in America, things became a lot more complicated, and it was no longer as simple as her being hunted by hitmen. The FBI were supposed to be protecting her, which technically, they were doing, but they were also using that protection as a façade to thwart her attempts to tell the truth about her research in Norway. There had to be a link to Diàoyú somewhere in all this tangled knot of lies and deception, but where the hell were they even meant to start?

She threw up her hands in frustration. "Ugh, this is impossible."

Jacob grabbed her hand and threaded his fingers between hers. "I know. We may never discern the motives of whomever is trying to hinder you. So, I think we need to stop attempting to figure it out and ask a better question. Which is, is there any way we might get you out of her so you *can* testify?"

She stared at him, wide-eyed. What was he thinking? "How can we hope to break out of here with four trained agents watching us? Listening to everything we say? We can't even contact anyone on the outside for help, so we're completely on our own. I don't have access to my notes because they have my computer, so I can't write up any evidence. And even if I did, what would be the point? I need to submit all my written proof at least a week before the trial, which is only two days away. And then, how the hell am I going to get all the way back to Norway? Are we going to just hijack an airplane?" Her voice took on a high-pitched squeak. The only thing stopping her from shouting in aggravation was Jacob's continued connection as he squeezed her hand

and the thought that the FBI might overhear her. "It's all so bloody frustrating," she finished in a hissed whisper.

"Frustrating, yes. But if we don't at least try, then they've already won." His gaze was clear and sure, filled with determination. A determination she wasn't feeling.

"You're right." Her shoulders sagged, and she dropped her head. "But where do we even start?"

"How about with contact with the outside world?" Jacob said thoughtfully. "Specifically, communication with your boss. Didn't you say you'd emailed him the raw data?"

"Yes." Nikki lifted her chin from her chest. "But how?"

"Do you have anything in this house that we could use to send a message? I'm assuming they've already searched this place for all electronic devices, but if you had something you kept hidden… Do you keep any of your old cell phones, perhaps?"

Nikki stood up, dropping his hand so she could cover her mouth to stop a squeak of delight from escaping. Why hadn't she thought of that? She was a hoarder when it came to outdated phones; she'd even kept her old Nokia, the first cell she'd ever owned, God knew why. There was a box full of all sorts of old technology, cables and cords and all those other things she knew she'd never use again but couldn't force herself to throw out. "Come with me." She dragged him out the door and down the hallway, hoping and praying they hadn't found her stash.

But when she stood on tiptoe so she could feel along the top shelf of the bookshelf in her office for the old shoebox that was always there, it was gone. Those bastards. Jacob had been right; they must've rifled through her house. The idea of a bunch of agents searching every inch of this building, hunting through every drawer—God, had they even searched her underwear drawer?—made her mad as hell. Even if she'd found a phone, none of them may have worked anyway, but that wasn't the point.

"It's gone," she whispered, wrinkling her nose in unhappiness, wanting to stamp her foot like a petulant child. How dare they go through her house, through all her belongings?

"Hmm, I thought as much," Jacob replied, his lips close to her ear. He looked as defeated as she felt. "You've got nothing else? An old computer or an iPad?" he asked, his voice so low she could barely make out what he was saying.

Nikki began to shake her head, but stopped as an idea struck. Her ancient iPad. She hadn't used it in years. Was there a chance they'd missed it? She refocused her mind on the large bookshelf that covered one wall of her office. It was stuffed full of books, mainly textbooks, but she was also an avid reader, and there were rows and rows of fiction, as well as biographies and even a stack of National Geographic magazines. Someone had searched through the bookshelf because they hadn't tried to hide the fingerprint marks they'd left in the dust on each shelf—she'd never been great at doing housework, and dusting was very low on her list of priorities.

Unerringly, she ran her finger down the spines of the works of fiction on the second lowest shelf, until she stopped at one that was thinner than most. She held back a shriek of triumph. It was still there; they hadn't found it because she kept it in a cute little cover that was made to look like a book. With a grin of delight, she withdrew the iPad and waved it over her head in a silent, joyous dance, then tucked it under her arm when she remembered they might have video surveillance in the room. She wanted to shout that those bloody FBI agents weren't as smart as they thought they were, but she held it in. Just. Jacob grinned from ear to ear when he saw it, and pulled her in for a big, bear hug.

Now they just had to pray that it still worked.

CHAPTER TWELVE

Jacob watched Nikki press send on the message she'd just composed to her boss, Russell, on the old iPad. They were sitting on the floor with their backs against Nikki's bed, whispering secretively, like two delinquent children who were about to be caught looking at porn any second. Except this was serious stuff. Life and death stuff.

She glanced over and their eyes locked, expressing her silent hopes without speaking. God, he hoped this worked. If not, he was just about out of options. The only plan B he could come up with consisted of him sneaking out of the house alone, avoiding detection, and he wasn't about to tell Nikki about that one, because he knew she'd try to stop him. And it was only a plan B if everything else failed; if he was caught escaping, the FBI might remove him completely and not allow him back in, leaving Nikki isolated, without protection. Which wasn't an option.

Agent Sabitino had rapped on the door a few hours earlier, and called out to see if they needed anything. Nikki had yelled back that if they would not return her computer and her phone, then they could all go to hell. Jacob had twitched the blind in the kitchen window aside and watched as Sabitino and Miller were relieved by two more agents, also dressed in civilian clothes. Jacob had stared at the red brake lights of the town car as it carried the two operatives away, deep in thought. Something about the agents was niggling at him. Was he being stupid, believing in false stereotypes, when he was under the impression that all FBI people wore dark, fitted suits? He'd never met a real FBI officer before, and so he guessed they could wear whatever they liked. But most cops he knew only ever wore plain clothes on the job when they were undercover. Were the agents who were assigned to Nikki's protection undercover? And if so, why?

Nikki wrote something on a notepad on the floor and slid it over to him. It said, *Now we wait and hope.* He crossed the fingers on both hands and held them up for her to see. Anything confidential they needed to say to each other was put in writing now. Jacob had surreptitiously checked the house for surveillance and found two video devices over the front and back doors, but in all other rooms he'd detected listening bugs only. It seemed the FBI were only worried about filming them if they tried to escape. He assumed all the entrances and windows were probably electronically alarmed, and although he could disarm one if necessary, he was by no means tech savvy and he might just set them off, which was one more reason plan B wasn't very good.

Nikki slid the iPad underneath her mattress and raised her shoulders as if to say, now what? It was after ten p.m., and the odds of Russell reading the message were slim. It'd taken them that long to cobble together a couple of cables that would allow them to charge up the ancient piece of tech, which hadn't been used in years. That it had even booted up was a miracle. Nikki had mainly used it to read eBooks, but it was so old that most of the software was no longer working. She found an app that was compatible with her iPad and that would also allow her to create a fake email address. Then they'd come up with a message using a code they hoped

Russell could decipher well enough to know it was from Nikki, but wouldn't raise any red flags if the FBI were monitoring his email. Now they had to hope and pray he wouldn't just delete the message as some kind of spam.

Jacob could think of a few things they could do to pass the time. All of them consisted of staying in Nikki's bedroom. Their lovemaking earlier had been a revelation. When she'd kissed him in the hallway and he'd given in to his wants, his desires, all the reasons he shouldn't be with her had become irrelevant. His job—which admittedly he might only be hanging onto by the thinnest of threads—the circumstances they were in, the fact she was a civilian witness he was supposed to be protecting, and that he lived in a far away country, all suddenly didn't matter. The only thing that was important was how she'd felt in his arms.

He leaned toward her, placed his hand on her cheek and turned her head so he could stare into her eyes. She considered him for a few seconds as he stroked her skin. Then she lifted her chin, her gaze never leaving his, and he bent his head to claim her mouth.

He did not know what lay in the future for them both, but for tonight, he wanted to be with this amazing woman one more time. Perhaps they could find sweet oblivion together.

She took him by the hand, pulling him off the floor, and they landed on her unmade bed, rolling in the still-rumpled sheets. Her arms twined around his neck, and he nuzzled her ear, drifting kisses up her jaw to claim her lips once more. He lifted the hem of her sweatshirt and floated a palm over her rib cage until he found her breasts. No bra. God, she was sexy. His cock surged at the thought. He cupped one breast, reveling in her small gasp of pleasure as his thumb stroked softly over her nipple. Raising his head, he watched her face as her eyes fluttered closed and she arched her back into his touch. Dark-blonde eyelashes brushed her perfect cheekbones as her tongue came out to wet her lips, and her long hair fanned out around her on the pillow.

She was the most beautiful woman he'd ever seen.

He'd understood that the very second he'd seen her standing naked in the sauna. It was true; every other woman he'd ever been with paled in comparison to Nikki. It wasn't just her physical beauty that struck a chord deep within his chest, however. She was just as beautiful on the inside as she was on the outside.

It was a ridiculous thought, but he couldn't banish the idea that perhaps he'd been waiting for Nikki all along.

His thoughts flashed back to the conversation they'd had earlier this evening. They'd been sitting at the kitchen table, celebrating the discovery of the iPad with a second cup of coffee and more toast. Nikki had placed her food on her plate and then said casually, "I should have asked this before we slept together, but we kind of got carried away." She gave him a little lopsided grin. "Do you have a girlfriend? Or a wife?" Her question had caught him by surprise. "Because if you do… I should probably know about it." She was right, of course; they should get this out in the open now before things went any further. Even if they weren't going to go any further, he owed her the truth.

But before he could answer, she held a hand in the air as if she was about to swear on a Bible. "Just so you know, I can solemnly promise you I am single. It's been a little over six months since I kicked my cheating bastard boyfriend, Bradley, out. And I haven't slept with anyone or even dated anyone until now."

Okay. That was good to know. He was a little taken aback at her casual tone, however, and he understood she was hiding a much deeper hurt beneath her flippancy, which needed to be addressed. But there were also a lot of other questions her seemingly simple comment raised. Like where was this bastard now? And would she like him to go over and teach him a lesson on how to treat women?

"But we can delve into my love life later," she said, lowering her hand. "Right now, I need an answer from you." She was still using that nonchalant tone, but there was a flash in her eyes of something deeply vulnerable as she stared at him. "Not that I'm asking for a commitment or anything like that. But…"

"Of course not," he said, his mind racing on how best to phrase his reply.

Women drifted in and out of his life like leaves carried on the wind. He seemed to attract a lot of female attention, which he enjoyed, but he never invited them to stay, and eventually they all left, some of them heartbroken, some just plain pissed at him. Nearly all of them had accused him of having a major fear of commitment, which he'd scoffed at loudly to anyone who would listen. Most recently, Freya had hinted that she wanted more from their liaison, but so far he'd carefully pretended to ignore her signals. It was only a matter of time before Freya dropped him completely, hoping to find someone who offered stability and fidelity instead of irregular booty calls. His girlfriend previous to Freya, a dark-haired beauty called Maria—they'd lasted almost a year together, a record for him—had done more than just hint, claiming he was a cold-hearted bastard when she'd stormed out of his door for the last time, which had stung. Even his sister, Rikka, had told him he treated women as disposable items, never seeing their true worth. She'd blamed their indifferent father and his callous disregard of his own children for how Jacob had turned out, and he hadn't argued. Because it could've been true. But maybe they'd all been wrong. Maybe now he knew why he'd never been able to commit to any of those other women.

Because none of them had been the right one.

"I have been seeing someone," he admitted, watching as Nikki's mouth formed into a thin line of dismay. "Her name is Freya. But it's a casual relationship, neither of us is committed. And the moment I slept with you, it was over." This was true, even if he hadn't told Freya yet. For him, it was over.

Jacob knew he owed it to Freya to tell her face to face. He would leave out the bit that their relationship had been over the moment he laid eyes on Nikki; that would just bring her even more hurt, and he didn't want that. Even though he and Freya had never said they would be monogamous, Jacob wasn't the type to sleep with more than one woman at a time, and so for him the choice was easy.

"Does Freya know it's over?" Nikki queried, and he'd grimaced.

"No, not yet." It was a hard admission to make, but even if he went back to Sweden and never saw Nikki again, he knew it would always be over with Freya; there was no comparison. "But I will tell her, I promise you that. I'm not a cheater."

Nikki had been quiet for a few moments, pondering his answer, but finally she'd lifted one eyebrow and said, "I believe you're a man of integrity. Unlike Bradley." He hated that her cheating ex-boyfriend had hurt her, and he scowled when he realized how easily she could put him in the same basket. "But if I find out you've lied to me later on...well, you'd better sleep with one eye open." She was joking, of course. But she said it with a sharp glint in her eye that made him wonder exactly what she might've had in mind if she found out he was indeed a philanderer. He wanted to tell her he would never do that to her. But he guessed his actions would speak louder than words; he just had to prove his worth as a man.

Nikki moved beneath him, pressing herself more firmly

into his palm and stifling a groan of pleasure, bringing him back to the present. He was so hard; he felt like he might explode. With his free hand, he undid his zipper and quickly shucked his jeans, then helped Nikki dispose of her sweatpants. No underwear either. The thought of her walking around all evening with nothing on under her clothes sent molten fire surging through his veins.

Then she touched him, and all logical thoughts fled as he shuddered with delight. Nothing mattered except for this erotic moment. He shed his T-shirt in a heartbeat, tugging her sweatshirt off as well, until they lay naked together, skin on skin.

"You're so damn beautiful," he breathed into her ear.

This time they made sure they did everything in complete silence, not wanting to give those FBI voyeurs anything. The cop part of Jacob knew the agents were merely doing their job, but it was still sick that someone would listen in on the intimate act of lovemaking, and so they delighted in giving nothing away. Having sex while being completely silent was new for him, and it added a certain edge, was perhaps even hotter than letting it all go. At one stage, Nikki covered her mouth with her own hand to stop herself from crying out, and that sent him into spirals of ecstasy as he stared down into her eyes, watching as she climaxed without uttering a sound.

Afterward, she lay in his arms, her breathing becoming slow and rhythmic. But he couldn't sleep. Instead, he studied Nikki in the sliver of light escaping through the curtains. He ran a gentle hand down the curve of her spine and over hips that jutted slightly. She was still thin—she'd told him later on in their frank discussion about commitment and ex-partners, that after her breakup with her ex, she'd lost weight due to stress. But she was stunning to him. Because it was her inner strength and compassion that called to him as much as her soft skin and wide, blue eyes. This woman made him feel like he was teetering on the very edge. Which scared him silly. But was exhilarating at the same time.

She was tough and resilient, determined to bring down this Chinese company that had killed her friends. Nikki's readiness to fight back caused his chest to swell with pride. The way she stubbornly refused to give up. But a small part of him wished she were a little more afraid. Because if she kept pushing, then she very well might end up dead. And that was one thing he couldn't bear to think of. Couldn't bear the thought of this world without her in it. Of her not being here, by his side. Which was confusing and a tad terrifying.

Whatever was between them was real, as real as he'd ever felt it.

Nikki twitched and then woke with a start.

"Oh, sorry, I was dreaming," she mumbled into his neck. He pulled her in closer.

She snuggled into him for a few seconds before suddenly pulling away. "Oh, I should check the—" She stopped herself just in time before she uttered the word iPad.

Reluctantly, he released her, but then enjoyed the sight of her climbing nude out of the bed. She hopped back in; the iPad clutched to her chest as she propped herself up on a pile of pillows. A sickly green glow lit up her gorgeous face as she opened the device. He sat up, watching her apprehensively. He saw the exact second she knew Russell had replied as her lips curled into a congratulatory smile, her eyes dancing with delight. She turned the screen so they could both read the email.

It was everything they'd hoped for and more. It seemed Russell was a man of conviction. He was going to help them. Jacob's mind immediately switched into analytical mode. This guy was going to be putting himself in danger. As were they all. So, he needed to make sure he got every detail planned down to the minutest detail, to keep them all safe.

* * *

Jacob stood on the front doorstep, toe to toe with Sabitino, Nikki straining like a dog on a leash to get past him. This was all part of the plan, but he wished Nikki wasn't playing her part quite so convincingly. If she pushed him any harder, he might have to physically restrain her. Miller wasn't anywhere to be seen, which was good. Two against one seemed to be a pretty fair fight. Weak morning sunlight washed over the porch, but the air was still icy, raising goosebumps on Jacob's bare arms, and he regretted he hadn't stopped to put on a jacket before opening the door.

"You need to let us out of here," he snarled. Sabitino was a few inches taller than Jacob, and it galled him he had to look up at the man. "You're violating our constitutional rights by keeping us here."

"Like I said, we're only trying to keep you safe," Sabitino retorted. The smug expression on Sabitino's face was turning the low simmering anger in Jacob's gut into a raging inferno. But he needed to maintain his cool.

"Bullshit you are," Nikki spat from behind Jacob's shoulder. She pushed against him, and he rocked on the balls of his feet before he leaned back into her; she was stronger than she looked. "You have to give me my computer and phone, you bastards." The pitch of Nikki's voice was rising, with a touch of hysteria in her tone. "I need to get out of here. You must let me go."

This time, Jacob stumbled forward a step as she pushed him again. Without taking his eyes off the agent in front of him, he half-turned so he could wrap his arms around Nikki. "It's okay. Let me handle this," he said firmly, but there was no need to act this time, because now he was worried she might just go barging out there, or even make a run for it down the steps and out of the front yard. But then he spotted

Miller at the end of the driveway as she stepped out from behind a large shrubbery and turned to look at them.

"No, these stupid assholes need to let us go. Tell them I don't want their stupid protection anymore," Nikki yelled, her voice loud enough to carry into the road. The agents wouldn't like the fact that she was making a scene. They would want to avoid attracting any attention, especially if they were conducting a sham operation, which Jacob suspected they were.

Sabitino narrowed his eyes and leaned forward. "All right, lady. Calm down. No need to get carried away." His words were muttered through clenched teeth, confirming Jacob's idea that he wanted to keep her quiet.

"No, I won't. They can't keep us here. They're not really FBI agents. I don't believe a word they're saying." She continued to rant. Jacob risked a glance at her face and saw actual tears in her eyes. She was taking this little showdown to heart. Then she shoved him so hard that he collided with Sabitino, who took three rapid steps backward, to the railing at the edge of the porch, his face suffusing with red.

"You both need to stop this right now," the agent snarled, the threat clear in his voice. Jacob heard Sabitino, but he was too busy trying to wrestle Nikki through the doorway to keep an eye on him. Nikki was doing a great job, but this was getting a little out of hand. He pushed her back gently, not wanting to hurt her, but she darted past him, and he only just snagged her around the waist in time before she flew at the FBI agent like an enraged lioness. Grunting with the effort, Jacob hauled her backward, shoving her inside. They'd come up with this plan late last night after receiving the reply from Russell, and up til now it was working well, but Nikki needed to take it down a notch or two before — "Agent Sabitino, stand down." It was Miller, Jacob could see her ascending the front steps out of the corner of his eye. Nikki suddenly stopped fighting him, her eyes going wide as she stared over his shoulder, and he pivoted in time to see Sabitino with his gun drawn, aimed straight at Jacob's head.

"What the fu—?" He turned and braced his body in the doorway facing Sabitino, forcing Nikki behind him. Jacob had pegged Sabitino as an arrogant hot-head, but even he had miscalculated this kind of overreaction. The other man had escalated the situation faster than Jacob could've imagined. A gunshot in this quiet neighborhood would arouse unwanted scrutiny, more so that just a few raised voices. He wondered why such a trigger-happy agent was even tolerated in the FBI. Surely they were taught to keep a cool head in this kind of circumstance.

"Stand down, Sabitino," Miller said again, her tone deep and authoritative. Her hand rested on the gun holster at her hip, her focus all on Sabitino as she ignored Nikki and Jacob. It was clear to Jacob that Miller would draw her gun on her partner if he didn't do as she commanded. The air sparked with tension as Sabitino continued to stare at Jacob, open hostility plain on his face. Then his mouth cracked with an insolent smile that didn't quite make it to his eyes as he holstered his weapon.

"What's going on here?" Miller asked, her fierce gaze flicking between him and Sabitino, her hand slowly dropping away from her holster.

"They were trying to break out of the house," Sabitino said, lowering his bushy eyebrows and flicking an imaginary piece of dust from his dark sports jacket.

"Were not," Nikki sputtered from behind him. "We were just telling him you can't keep us here without our consent. It's called kidnapping, and—"

"We want to see Linstead," Jacob cut in before Nikki could add any more fuel to the fire. "Make it happen," he said, gaze narrowing in on the female agent. "Or else." He wasn't sure what *or else* meant, but she needed to know he wasn't joking. She would get the message through. The big oaf Sabitino just wanted to fight. But Miller had the intelligence and the foresight to recognize when to capitulate. And when to bring in the big guns.

"I'll talk to him," Miller agreed, her lips forming a firm line of resolution.

"Make it today. Soon," Jacob shot back at her, meeting her dark gaze with his own. She gave an infinitesimal nod of her head, and Jacob knew they'd won this round. Without another word, he bustled Nikki inside the house and slammed the door in the agent's faces.

"What the hell was that?" he mouthed silently at her as they stood in the dim hallway, his back toward the video camera.

She shrugged and whispered, "Improvisation. I thought I was pretty good."

Good? She'd been great. Scarily so. They'd achieved their first goal. Now, hopefully, the rest of the plan went just as smoothly.

He grappled Nikki into a bear hug, then kissed her hard, claiming her, desperate to feel her warm, stubborn mouth on his. Closing his eyes for a second as he tasted her sweetness, his spike of adrenaline receded. She was fine. They were both fine. But he needed to feel her whole and alive pressed against his chest before the last of his heightened anxiety levels came back to normal. They were taking a calculated risk here, but things could still go terribly wrong. Especially if Nikki decided to go off script. Because if he couldn't control her, then he couldn't control the situation, and that might be a path to ruination. But right now, he was happy just to revel in the feel of her mouth against his.

CHAPTER THIRTEEN

Nikki paced across the kitchen, the aging wooden floorboards squeaking beneath her socked feet. She stopped when she reached the sink, peered out the window for a few seconds, then turned and continued pacing. Where was Linstead? It'd been two hours since their little pantomime on the front porch. Jacob assured her that Linstead would come; they just didn't know when. She'd already checked the window beside the back door in the washroom, twice, and the same agent—the driver from their car from the airport the other day—was still in his position outside, ambling slowly up and down the concrete pathway that led to her garden shed, stopping now and then to stomp his feet. She almost felt sorry for him; it must be a cold, thankless job standing guard for endless hour after hour. Almost sorry, but not enough to really care—he was just another jailer after all. There was no sign of the second operative stationed out the back, but he had to be out there somewhere, doing a circuit of the yard, or perhaps hiding behind some bushes, not wanting to make it too obvious there was a phalanx of agents surrounding her residence, so as not to alert the neighborhood there was something fishy going on.

After three more fruitless circuits of the kitchen, Jacob

reached out and grabbed her hand as she walked past where he was seated at the small table, stopping her forward motion. He frowned at her but didn't articulate his thoughts because everything they said was being monitored. Now she knew how a caged lion must feel. This helpless waiting was just about killing her.

But she gave Jacob a wan smile and took a seat at the table, more to appease him than because she wanted to. They sat in uneasy silence, she unable to think of any small talk to lighten the mood. Resisting the urge to look out the window one more time, she propped her elbows on the countertop and nibbled on her nails. Which was most unlike her; she never chewed her nails, not even when she was terribly stressed. She'd always thought she was one cool customer. But this was a whole other level of stress, one she'd never encountered before.

Lost in her thoughts, she almost hit the ceiling when a loud knock sounded at the front door and she leapt out of her chair to head into the hallway. But Jacob beat her to it. He motioned for her to stay back, that he would let the agent in and to just stay calm. This had to be Linstead. It was the exact thing they'd been waiting for, but now he was here, Nikki wondered if she could go through with it.

A low buzz of conversation filled the passage, then a few moments later, Agent Linstead rounded through the kitchen door, Jacob hot on his heels, with Miller right behind him. They'd expected that Linstead wouldn't enter the house alone, and she was glad it was the female agent and not that hot-headed asshole, Sabitino. Drawing in a deep, controlling breath, Nikki kept her face passive as Linstead shot her a ready smile. Their self-appointed prison officer didn't deserve any kind of welcome. His grin faltered only slightly as he caught her look of contempt. The room was crowded now with the four of them all milling around.

"I heard you wanted to see me," Linstead opened the conversation as he pulled out a chair and sat, crossing his legs with careful consideration and dusting off a speck on non-existent fluff, clearly feeling superior and totally unconcerned. Well, he was about to find out the hard way not to mess with her. And Jacob. Miller remained standing in the main doorway, her usual cool, unruffled self. Nikki secretly hated that the woman never seemed to have a hair out of place; it was always pulled back into a simple ponytail that on anyone else would've looked severe, but on Miller just highlighted her high cheekbones and startling green eyes. She would be stunning under the right circumstances.

Jacob leaned casually against the countertop a few feet away from Miller, seemingly also unconcerned, which left Nikki standing on the opposite side of the table to Linstead, with her back to the doorway that led to the washroom.

But before she could jump into their rehearsed conversation, Jacob surprised her by asking, "Where's Sabitino? And who's the new bloke out on the front porch?"

Linstead shot him an unfathomable look. "Sabitino has been reassigned," he said.

Wow, that was interesting. She risked a glance in Jacob's direction, and he raised a sardonic eyebrow. After the showdown on the porch, they'd retreated to her bathroom to regroup without the surveillance watching them. They'd only stayed a few minutes, not wanting to raise too many suspicious, just enough time for him to hold her tight until the adrenaline had faded and she stopped shaking. Then he'd whispered into her ear while they ran the faucet that Sabitino's reaction had been over the top, and they needed to watch out for him. But if his assessment was correct, and this team was working outside of normal channels, then these FBI officers were trying to keep everything on the low-down. And Sabitino's little scene had been the exact opposite of discreet. The agent's sudden removal seemed to support his theory.

"But that's not why you called me in here, is it?" Linstead's cool, gray eyes landed on Nikki, and she drew in a lungful of air, readying herself.

"No, it's not. We believe you're holding us illegally. I want to talk to a lawyer." She put her hands on her hips to hide the fact that they were shaking, and faced him across the table, piercing him with her best icy stare. God, she hoped she could do this. A small part of her wondered if Jacob's faith in her acting abilities had been misplaced. She was suddenly unsure she could see this through.

"I'm sorry, that's not possible," Linstead replied easily. "Your friendly Swedish cops still haven't caught the two men who were trying to kill you, and we now have no idea where they are. They could very well be hunting you down right here in the US. We are doing this to keep you safe," he stated, spreading his hands in what she assumed was a gesture of goodwill, but it only made her blood begin to boil.

"I don't believe you," Nikki countered. Linstead smiled in return and said nothing. "Well then, at least tell me when you're going to release us." Even though this was all scripted, Nikki could feel her anger rising; she wanted to slam her fist down on the table in a fit of pique. And why the hell not, she decided. The smack as her hand hit the wood was very satisfying, and it even had Miller taking a step forward. Jacob didn't move a muscle, but Nikki could tell by the tiny crease in his forehead that he was readying himself. "If you really are just keeping us *'safe'*," she raised her hands and made air quotes above her head, "then will you let us go on the day that the trial starts?"

Linstead stared at her and pursed her lips. His cool indifference got right under her skin. He was probably used to staying in control under pressure; he was an FBI agent after all, and she'd do well not to forget it. But right now his complete lack of concern was playing right into her scheme, because she could feel her face flushing with the injustice of her situation. And the madder she got, the more unhinged she became, the more believable this would all look, and the less nervous she was.

"Or will it be the day after I'm supposed to give my testimony?" She demanded. "So that when I don't turn up, the judge shall be forced to move on?" She was getting a good head of steam up now, could feel the blood beginning to surge, hot and heavy in her veins. Leaning both hands on the table, she glared at Linstead. "Or will it be once the court case is finished? Which could take weeks, months even." She thumped the table again for added emphasis. "I will not stay locked up in here for months." A bit of spittle flew out of her mouth and landed on the tabletop between them.

Linstead kept his eyes trained on her, but she could see his barely hidden contempt. He didn't care one bit about her predicament, or that a big Chinese company was going to be allowed to continue raping and pillaging pristine ocean waters. She was a job to him, nothing more. He didn't care about her, and he certainly didn't care about the environment, something she was passionate about, something she'd given her whole life to protecting. It was that realization that tripped the switch inside her, and much like it had out on the front porch this morning, she sensed an anger like she'd never felt before.

She used that rage, twisted it to suit herself. If she looked half-crazy now, then perhaps it was because she was.

"I'm sorry, I really am, but—" Linstead began, but she cut him off, yelling now.

"And what about my friend's funeral? I want to go to Tammy's funeral. I need to be there to say goodbye. You can't keep me here." She ended her tirade with a sob. A real sob—

she didn't need to fake it—the thought of missing Tammy's funeral hit her with the force of a punch. It was true; she needed to bid farewell to her friend, but she knew this bastard would not allow it. That belief banished all doubt from her head. She could do this because she had to. For her friends if not for herself.

Linstead pushed back in his chair, but didn't rise, content to stay seated, arrogant enough to think she wouldn't be a problem. Miller wasn't so complacent, and though Nikki had her full focus on Linstead, she saw the agent take another step toward her in her peripheral vision.

Linstead spoke. "Like I said, I'm really sorry, but I have my orders. If it were up to me—"

"That's all bullshit," Nikki screeched. "You're lying. You have to let me out of here. I need to get out of here." Miller moved closer again, and Jacob stood up from where he'd been lounging against the countertop.

It was now or never.

Nikki pushed the table hard toward Linstead, and at the same time Jacob took Miller in a grapple hold around the neck. Then all hell broke loose. Nikki screamed something incoherent and made a dash for the door behind her that led to the washroom.

She heard Linstead curse, then yell, "Bakshi, get in here." The small part of her mind that wasn't overtaken by near hysteria registered that he must be calling in the new agent from the front, which meant she only had a few seconds. It was a quirk of her house that not many people knew about. Unlike most other wash rooms which normally led straight out to the rear door, hers had a second door cut into it, exiting back into the hallway right next to her bedroom. The door had already been there when she'd first moved in, and at first she thought about filling it in. But then she noticed how useful it was, because instead of having to detour all the way down the passage and right through the kitchen when she carried her load of clothes from her bedroom to the washer, she could just duck through the semi-secret entrance. Most people would assume that the door hid a closet behind it, and wouldn't give it a second glance.

Now, she lunged for the concealed door, yanking it open and letting herself into the hallway. At the other end, the front entrance was open, and a dark figure loomed in the doorway; Bakshi. The sounds of a scuffle emanated from the kitchen as Jacob contended with Linstead and Miller, trying to block them from getting to her. She had only seconds to complete her mission. Her socks slipped on the polished wooden floors, and she cursed her lack of thought about her unsuitable footwear as she scrambled to open the door to her bedroom. Loud footsteps boomed on the floorboards behind her.

She raced around her bed in the middle of the room, almost colliding with her chest of drawers as she skidded on the shiny boards again. Crashing into the little table that sat beneath her window, she sent two picture frames flying, praying they wouldn't break as they hit the floor. Her fingers unfastened the window lock, and she threw it open, climbing up onto the table and swinging one leg up over the windowsill.

She was almost free; she'd almost made it.

As soon as she cracked the window open, she could hear some kind of alarm sound in the house, but she ignored it and tried to swing her other leg out the opening.

Then a muscular arm came around her waist, hauling her inside and tossing her onto the bed as if she weighed nothing.

"Where do you think you're going, missy?" The large man she'd seen in the doorway now loomed over her, but didn't touch her again. Linstead appeared out of breath, his hair tousled and out of place. Where was Jacob? Perhaps he was still wrestling with Miller. She hoped he was okay. But there was no time to consider him; they were both playing a part, and she needed to complete hers.

"Let me go. I want out. You have to let me go," she wailed incessantly. Lashing out with her feet, she landed a kick squarely in the big man's groin and heard a satisfying howl of pain. That bit hadn't been rehearsed, but she was quite proud of her quick thinking.

Now she just needed to execute the last part of their plan.

With an athletic leap that impressed even her, she flew off the bed and plowed into Linstead, trying to push past him. For some unknown reason—perhaps he was still off balance from his dash from the kitchen—she crash tackled her way into him, knocking him to the floor, and then she was in the hallway, with the wide-open front exit beckoning to her.

She could be out of that door and down the steps before anyone caught her. Run across the road and knock on her neighbors, Steve and Heather's, door. Steve would be home from work by now; he'd protect her.

She could be free.

But that wasn't the plan. And she needed to stick to the plan. Because even if she got free, Jacob would be left behind. A loud grunt of pain sounded from the kitchen, and she recognized it as Jacob, just as the back door burst open and she heard booted feet thumping on the floorboards. Linstead had regained his feet and was reaching for her. Jacob would be overpowered in a second, possibly hurt or beaten if she didn't do something.

Just as Linstead's iron fist clamped around her bicep, Nikki crumpled to the floor in a dead faint.

CHAPTER FOURTEEN

Jacob was so proud of her, his chest felt like it was exploding. Nikki had fulfilled the brief and more with her beautiful performance. She would've made a great cop, he decided as he cradled her in his arms. They were on the couch in the living room, her head in his lap, pretending she'd fainted as Linstead ranted from the doorway. At least he hoped she was faking. Because she was doing an excellent job of it.

Nikki cracked an eyelid open and quirked a knowing eyebrow, then shut it again quickly as Miller came in carrying a glass of water, and he almost grinned with relief. He took the proffered glass and lifted Nikki into a half-sitting position.

"Come on, babe, have a drink. It'll make you feel better," he pleaded. She moaned something incomprehensible, but sat up straighter, opening her eyes and taking a greedy sip of water. *Good girl.* She was playing her role to perfection.

"Bakshi," Linstead snapped. The new agent tore his gaze away from Jacob and Nikki to stare at his boss from his vantage point in the corner of the room. If Jacob wasn't mistaken, Bakshi had been enjoying the spectacle of Nikki's meltdown and escape attempt. The guy probably didn't get much action on any normal given day. "Make sure that damn window is shut, then get back out to the front porch and check no one in the neighborhood heard that commotion."

"Yes, sir." Bakshi skirted past his boss and headed down the hallway, giving one last glance in Nikki's direction as he went.

Linstead had stabbed at his phone a few moments ago, turning the blaring siren off. At least Jacob now knew the windows were indeed alarmed, and the notification went straight to Linstead. The other agent who'd been on guard out the back had already returned to his station, having not been needed in the end.

"Come on," Jacob urged, giving Nikki a gentle shake. "Another sip for me."

She groaned again, and this time sat up completely. "Where am I?" she asked in a bewildered tone. Then her gaze landed on Linstead, and she said, "You," in such a menacing tone Linstead looked up from his phone. "Get out of my house. Now!" She lifted an imperious finger and pointed straight at his heart.

Linstead opened his mouth, probably about to utter a placation, but Nikki got in first.

"Don't you dare say another word," she growled. "Get out of my house, you…you…monster, or I'll start screaming, and I won't stop until the entire neighborhood comes running."

Linstead shut his mouth with a click and glared at Nikki. But her threat had him wavering; Jacob had been right, the less attention they drew to this house, the better. Instead, he turned his focus to Jacob. "You need to keep your woman on a leash," he said, and Jacob knew they were finally seeing the true Linstead. Jacob had suspected there was a nasty side to the man. "I won't be so lenient if this happens again." He turned on his heel and with a swift gesture for Miller to follow him, headed toward the door. Miller gave them both one hasty, appraising glance before she went after him. Miller was much more astute than Linstead, and Jacob hoped she hadn't just smelled something fishy in their little performance.

"Good riddance," Nikki yelled after him. "Come on, I need a shower to wash this filth off me," she stated loudly, staring after Linstead's retreating back. The front door slammed, shaking the whole house on its foundations, leaving a heavy silence behind.

"Are you really okay?" he asked, not having to fake his concern. Her face was pale but determined. And so beautiful that it made his heart squeeze just looking at her. He wanted to kiss her until they both ran out of breath, could feel the life pumping through her veins, set her alight with his desire; the idea someone might be listening in was the only thing stopping him.

"Yes." She nodded, then got to her feet. "But I really do need that shower."

Without letting go of her hand, he followed dutifully into the bedroom. But rather than heading to the bathroom, she made a beeline for the now-closed window. Jacob saw two photo frames lying on the floor, with the glass smashed. Nikki ignored the broken pictures, instead kneeling down and opening the top drawer of the small table. She made a squeaking sound of triumph, which she instantly quashed, but when she turned around, she was brandishing a laptop in one hand and a dongle in the other. Russell had come through. Their plan had worked.

All that subterfuge had been staged to achieve just one goal. Once Nikki had turned on her hysterical scene, drawing all attention to her and away from the front garden, then got that window open, and re-directed all the agents' focus away from her bedroom and back to the main lounge area, Russell had time to sneak around the front of the house, reach in through the window and deposit the computer and the Wi-Fi device, and then hightail it out of there before anyone was the wiser. Simple but effective. All they'd needed was a diversion, and Nikki had provided that perfectly.

She now had the wherewithal to analyze the data she and her colleagues had collected, then capture it all in a document that she could send to the prosecutors in charge of the court case. And she had two days to do it. Russell was helping as much as he could. He would be her intermediary, liaising with the lawyers, letting them know what was going on. She was counting on him to negotiate a video link-up for her testimony, rather than an in-person appearance. This was going to take some wrangling, as it was unusual in a high-profile case such as this for the expert witness not to be there in the flesh. They had to keep their fingers crossed Russell could convince the prosecution to get the judge to agree, because there was no way Nikki was about to get onto a commercial airline and fly to Oslo, not with half the FBI in America on her tail. But if they could wrangle this just right, she might be able to get to some place safe and hunker down long enough to give her statement via video link.

And that would have to be sufficient. There was nothing else she could do.

Nikki quickly slipped the computer and dongle under the mattress—the same hiding place as her ancient iPad—then stood and took him by the hand, leading him into the bathroom without a word. Her eyes told him all he needed to know. The shower might've been a ploy to go back to her room, but she was going to make sure they both enjoyed their ablutions.

They celebrated their victory by stripping each other naked and exploring each other's bodies under the hot spray. Now he could kiss her however and wherever he desired, and he did exactly that. Using his lips to tell her how much he cared. How much he wanted her. A want like none he'd ever experienced before. No other woman had quite this effect on him. Desperate desire mixed with something painfully pure and yet intangible.

Lathering up the soap, he used his slick palm to wander over her curves and long limbs, flat stomach and then down to the V between her legs. He gloried in all that soft, creamy skin, learning the lines of her body, the rhythm of her beating heart as he teased with his fingers, then his mouth. She arched her back when his hands found her breasts, her eyes going dark with desire. Nails dug into his shoulders, the light scrape sending an erotic pulse through to his cock. Her mouth was wet and hot, demanding on his. He took her up against the wall, covering her mouth to stop her crying out as he plunged into her over and over, then watched her face as her orgasm pushed her soaring over the edge to oblivion. Only then did he allow himself to follow, the force of his own climax leaving him shuddering and weak at the knees, so that he had to grab hold of the showerhead to prevent them both tumbling to the tiled floor.

Afterward, once they dried off and snuggled beneath the blankets of her bed to keep warm, he nuzzled her neck and whispered in her ear, telling her how beautiful she was. That she was a lioness, so courageous and fierce, standing up to Linstead and his cronies. She smiled and stroked his face as they lay facing each other, and he knew a moment of such pure joy that he was almost speechless.

But soon, reality overtook them. She had a job to do, as did he. His job was to protect her as she wrote up her testimony, not let anyone discover what they were up to. And to come up with a plan so that she could fulfill her wish to appear via video link at that court case. That was still a week away, but whatever they did to escape this house, it'd have to be foolproof. The FBI weren't dummies, and Jacob wasn't stupid enough to believe this was going to be easy. But he'd do everything in his power to make it happen. Because of her. Because he believed in her. Because she meant a great deal to him.

Before he could explore that thought any more, Nikki sat up and stretched, revealing those delectable breasts as the sheet fell away. She gave a loud yawn, and announced, "I'm tired, I think I'll sleep for a while."

"Good. I'll make dinner, you just rest," he suggested loudly, easing himself out of bed and going to the bathroom to salvage his clothes. "I'll wake you up in a few hours," he said as he returned and slipped his T-shirt over his head. She merely nodded, watching him with anxious eyes as he retrieved the electronics from their hiding place at the end of the bed and as quietly as possible handed them over to her with a conspiratorial grin. She took a deep breath, then grinned back at him. But as she opened the computer, her smile fell away, and her brow furrowed as she turned all her focus to the task ahead. Jacob watched her for a few moments, the sickly green light from the screen turning her face almost ghostly.

This was the only safe place for Nikki to write to make sure her captors couldn't see what she was up to. The Wi-Fi dongle allowed her unimpeded access to the internet and also made sure the FBI couldn't track what she was doing. They'd taken a chance sending the first email to Russell through her home Internet connection because the FBI were likely monitoring her usage. It seemed they had got away with it, however, as there had been no repercussions and no questions asked. Now, she'd have to sit in bed and type quietly, but it was the only way she was going to get anything done. He left her to it, hoping that by making enough noise and mess in the kitchen, he'd divert the attention of anyone who was watching or listening onto his antics, and not what she was up to in the bedroom.

CHAPTER FIFTEEN

Nikki stood, yawned, stretched and ambled over to the kitchen window. On the outside, she needed to act bored and perhaps a tad frustrated. Hiding how she was truly feeling on the inside, which was like a boiling cauldron of oil about to spill over and scorch everything in its path.

Tonight was the night.

She was supposed to appear via video link to a packed courtroom in Oslo.

Everything was in place; they just had to wait for exactly the right moment. Which would be soon. Very soon.

Jacob looked up from the book he'd been reading at the kitchen table and gave a wan smile. She ambled over and draped an arm around his shoulders, pretending to lean down and read from the book he held in his hands. Jacob seemed as relaxed and bored as she did, but when she touched him, the muscles in his back were so tense they felt like they were molded from iron; a dead giveaway as to the true anxiety humming through his body. It was nearly midnight, and the sky was cold and full of snow outside. They'd had a late dinner, and Nikki had made sure to eat all of it, even though her stomach rebelled at the thought, because she'd need all her strength for what was about to come.

It'd been nine days since Russell had smuggled the computer in. And in that time, there'd been no more escape attempts. No more meltdowns. Nikki had behaved like someone who'd been beaten into submission. Someone who'd accepted her fate. Jacob had spent many hours in the few days after they'd received the laptop painstakingly explaining why she could never try that kind of thing again. How she might've got herself killed, and how their best chance now was just to play the waiting game. She needed to stop believing that she was going to change the world. That one stupid court case wasn't enough for them to lose their lives over. And besides, he was sure Linstead was a man of his word and would let them out once the trial was finished, and then they could resume their lives.

It'd all been a show, of course. Jacob played the logical, practical cop, while she played the hysterical damsel in distress who realized the error of her ways, then finally agreed that she would behave. But behind the scenes she'd been madly analyzing and writing and thinking and strategizing. Those first two days after she'd got her hands on the computer, she'd spent a lot of time in bed *recovering*. The ordeal had been too much for her and she'd used that excuse to stay in her bedroom, to *pull herself together* after Linstead's cruel treatment while Jacob talked her down, but in truth she was writing, while he covered the sound of her typing with his unceasing monologue.

She'd sent her notes off to Russell with a few hours to spare before the deadline. The official statement wasn't up to her normal standards, but all the pertinent points were there, and hopefully the judge would allow her to elaborate on the day so she could push her point across. And her point would be that Diàoyú Aquaculture was openly flaunting Norwegian rules and regulations governing its plastic waste pollution. It was damning evidence, and exactly what the Norwegian government wanted to hear. There would be other expert witnesses, of course, looking at the health of the fish, the quality of the final product for human consumption due to an elevated level of disease, the quality of the water surrounding the farms and effect on wild marine flora and fauna populations because of high fecal loads, that kind of thing. But her testimony could be the final nail in the coffin that ended the Chinese company's fish farming days forever in Norwegian waters. If it were proven the fish farming company was not adhering to protocol, then it was actively breaking the law. Which was why Diàoyú had been so determined to get rid of Tammy, Antoine, and Nikki. But they'd sorely underestimated her. And Jacob. She and Jacob together were a force to be reckoned with.

This court case might not stop this Chinese company from setting up its farms elsewhere around the world, but Nikki hoped that other countries were watching and learning, and would halt the practice once and for all. Or at the very least make sure these companies were held accountable to mandatory regulations and management from now on.

The past week had been a lesson in self-control. Showing one face to the cameras and listening devices, while keeping their actual conversations secret, only talking freely in the shower. Which'd been highly frustrating. Sometimes she'd forget and open her mouth to ask Jacob about a detail that'd been bugging her and then have to change tack halfway through her sentence when she realized what she'd said. Jacob had a plan, but because they only had snatched moments here and there to talk it through, she was more vague on the details than she'd like.

At least her house was now spotless. She'd taken the hours of boredom and turned them into a cleaning frenzy. She'd even spring-cleaned the kitchen cupboards and her own wardrobe, handing over bags of unwanted items to Miller through a crack in the front door for her to get rid of. Miller had tried to start up conversations with Nikki, but she'd stone-walled the agent, only answering in mono-syllables and only if it were truly necessary. Miller had betrayed her, as had the other FBI agents who were in on this farce of a protection detail, and Nikki would never forgive that.

The one bright spark in the endless week had been Jacob. They made love every night, under the cover of darkness, muffling their cries of ecstasy with a pillow or a hand, but sometimes she was so overcome nothing would stop her. And right then she didn't care if the world knew that she and Jacob were having sex. Lots of sex. Good sex. Great sex. Phenomenal even. Gosh, he was good at sex.

It was the one thing she didn't want to end. But today everything was going to change, and she had no idea where they went from here. What did the future hold for the two of them? Her arm tightened around his shoulders, drawing him in, feeling the strength of him.

Raised voices sounded from the front driveway.

They were here.

Jacob looked up from his book, straight into her eyes. And she knew this was it.

Everything was ready. Her backpack was stashed in the back of the wardrobe with the computer and iPad and everything else she might need.

All she had to do was get her shoes and jacket on.

Quick.

But she didn't want to let go of Jacob, and as he stood, she clung to him. He stared down into her eyes, and she felt a sudden lump form in her throat. So many words unsaid that wanted to erupt from her mouth, but they were out of time.

The voices got louder, and Nikki could hear chanting.

It was another simple plan that, if carried out correctly,

would see her and Jacob free.

Russell had recruited every member of the Marine Institute, his family and all his friends and told them to congregate out the front of Nikki's house and demand to be let in to see her. Oslo was nine hours ahead of them here in Seattle and she was due to take the virtual stand at one p.m. tonight, which also played into their favor; the FBI wouldn't be expecting anything to happen at midnight on this sleepy street on a Monday night. Jacob hoped that the sheer size of numbers would render the FBI agents ineffective; they wouldn't be able to shoot over a hundred people all at once, and more to the point, they wouldn't dare. These were law-abiding, innocent civilians. If the agents tried to blast their way out and killed or wounded even one person, their careers would be over. Linstead and Miller were smart enough to understand that the moment they were confronted with the mob. Sabitino might not have been so cognizant, and may have shot first and asked questions later, but he was out of the picture, so all the better.

"Go on," he said, staring down into her eyes. "You're ready. We're ready. Let's get out of here." He took her shoulders as he leaned in to kiss her on the lips. Passionate and deep, as if he were putting his stamp on her, claiming her, letting her know how much she meant to him. Then he pushed her gently back, and his eyes hardened as his gaze left hers and sharpened on the scene through the kitchen window. "Go," he said again, this time not looking at her. "I'll see you at the rendezvous, just like we planned."

Unable to talk past the increasing lump in her throat, she merely nodded. Drawing away from Jacob, already missing the feel of his big body against hers, she watched as he grabbed a chair and made his way into the hallway to bar the front door. She wondered whether this was all worth the risk. They were putting their lives on the line today. She almost called him back. But then Tammy and Antoine's sacrifice would all be for nothing. Then Diàoyú would win. And that wasn't an option.

Grabbing another of the kitchen chairs, she dragged it through to the laundry, taking a fleeting glance out of the little window next to the rear door as she did so. And saw people, lots and lots of people, dark shapes in the dark night, flooding down the driveway around the side of her house, filling up the backyard. In the glare of the single spotlight lighting up her porch, she could see the FBI agents shouting and waving their guns, but Nikki didn't have time to stop and make sure everyone was okay. She had her assignment. The chair was solid wood, and she jammed it up under the back door handle, stopping anyone from entering the house, knowing Jacob had done the same thing with the front. None of the agents could get in this way unless they had a ramrod, or she let them in.

Task done, she almost wavered, wanting to watch everything unfold outside. But this was her chance. She couldn't fail them all now, not when so many people had come to her aid. Her heart swelled as the image stayed with her while she rushed through the hidden doorway into her bedroom and the enormity of what was occurring hit her. This crowd was here for her—or, more accurately, because of Russell—but to help her cause none-the-less.

Quickly and silently, Nikki donned her shoes, her jacket and retrieved her backpack from the rear of the wardrobe and was back in the hallway in under thirty seconds. She took a precious few moments to study Jacob's back as he stood tall and silent at the other end, by the front door, all his focus directed through the peephole as he watched the unfolding event outside. Miller was banging on the door, demanding to be let in, but Jacob ignored her, bracing all his weight against the chair as she battered it harder and harder.

Taking a mental snapshot of his broad-shouldered figure, she stored it away for later, then she went back to the laundry room and stood behind the door, leaning around the side so she could peek out of the small window. The backyard was now crammed with people. It wasn't a big yard, and the corners remained dark where the spotlight didn't reach, but there must be at least eighty or ninety individuals out there. Nikki wondered if her front yard looked the same, because if it did, then her neighbors were definitely coming out onto the sidewalk even this late at night for a look. So much for Linstead wanting to keep this on the down low. Nikki would love to see him explain this away to his superiors.

The crowd in her backyard were all chanting at the top of their voices, *"Let her go, let her go,"* and they were drowning out any chance that the two FBI agents would be heard over the hubbub. One agent was backed right up against the door; she could see his left shoulder through the window. He was brandishing his gun in the air, but wasn't aiming it at anyone, and even Nikki could tell it was all bluff. He'd probably tried to get inside already, but the chair was holding fast. Such an old trick, but a good one; it'd been Jacob's idea. The second FBI agent was at the rear of the yard, with his back up against her small garden shed. He was only just keeping the crowd at bay by strong-arming anyone who came into his personal space, pushing them back. This man—Nikki had never found out his name—had already admitted defeat and had holstered his weapon, but was still yelling at people to get away from him.

Her escape was imminent, but she needed the guy by the door to move; otherwise, she was stuck. She scanned the faces of the throng who were gathered at the bottom of the steps, chanting in unison and pointing at the agent who'd come to his senses and also put his gun away, but then pulled out a taser and pointed it menacingly at them. Nikki didn't know who all these folks were. Russell must've called in every favor from every individual from every walk of life he'd ever known in his fifty-one years.

A face she recognized morphed out of the crowd in the second row of chanting individuals. Dr. Reshma Siram was a conservation analyst working at the Marine Institute. Nikki had consulted with her a few times when she'd been trying to decipher her results from various field trips. The woman was young, but highly intelligent, and while they weren't close friends, Nikki respected her shrewd mind, even if it were hidden beneath an unassuming exterior. They locked gazes, her colleague's face all sharp angles and shadows from the bright spotlight. Using sign language, she pointed at the agent outside her door and made shooing motions. Would she understand what Nikki needed? Reshma pushed her bifocals higher up her nose and bit her bottom lip for a second. Her long, black hair swayed over her shoulders as she considered the people on either side of her. Then, as if coming to a decision, Reshma gave Nikki the thumbs up, and Nikki held her breath.

For a second, Reshma disappeared into the crowd, and Nikki wondered if the woman was going to renege on her undertaking. But then she popped up a little way along the line beside a very tall man with a very thick neck and tattooed biceps that bulged out of his tight t-shirt. Reshma whispered in his ear until the guy raised his head and nodded, an excited gleam in his eyes. Nikki watched as Reshma moved through the group, recruiting four more of the biggest guys she could find, who all looked at the agent at the top of the stairs with heightened interest as they nodded enthusiastically.

Then with a loud yell that was most unlike the Reshma that Nikki knew, the woman erupted through the crowd and rushed up the steps, straight at the FBI officer. Did Reshma have no fear? Had she lost her mind? Or did she not realize the magnitude of what she was doing? This wasn't the dutiful and docile person Nikki knew. A diminutive Indian lady going up against a bull of an agent in a black hoodie waving a taser in her face. This was no contest, surely? Nikki was terrified for Reshma; she was going to get hurt, and it would all be Nikki's fault.

But then the five handpicked men all came roaring out of the crowd behind her, charging up the steps like a human storm. There was a loud scuffle, and Nikki cursed the solid wooden door that stopped her from seeing everything that was happening. A man screamed in pain, and there was a loud thump as something heavy landed on the wooden deck. The rest of the throng surged forward, more of them running up the steps. The loud grunts and screams increased until it sounded like a full-on melee outside her door. Then everything went quiet.

Nikki strained to see what was going on through the small side window, but all she could make out was a tangle of bodies on her back porch, twisting and heaving. Nikki had had enough; she needed to see what was going on. She wrestled with the chair under the doorknob, shoving it aside and wrenching the door open.

The pile of humans was still writhing on her back deck, but one at a time, someone disentangled themselves from the mound, then stood back to help pull others out of the heap, until at last Reshma's original big men were revealed. Each of them grunted and heaved their way upright, and then there was only a solitary man left lying on the porch. The agent was unconscious, knocked out cold. One of the big men, the tattooed bald man, was on his knees, glaring at the agent as if he wanted to kill him. Someone helped him to his feet, but he remained unsteady, leaning heavily on the good Samaritan.

Reshma pushed her way through the milling crowd until

she stood in front of Nikki. "You're free." She beamed a hundred-watt smile and repositioned her glasses back up her nose.

"Yes, thanks to you." Nikki was very unsure what'd just happened, but she didn't have time to stand around and chat. "I'm still not safe," she said, lifting her chin and indicating the other agent who'd been pinned next to the shed, but was pushing frantically at the crowd now, slowly forging his way toward her.

"Oh, yes, right," Reshma answered brusquely. "Come with me, then." Who was this woman? She looked like the Reshma Nikki knew from the Institute, but that's where the similarity ended. It was as if she'd been transformed into someone else, the way she cleared a path with an imperious wave of her hand, drawing Nikki after her and guiding her away as if she'd somehow become the crowd's self-appointed leader and was relishing the role.

Nikki wondered what was going on at the front door? Was Jacob faring as well as she just had? His job had been to stop anyone coming in for as long as was humanly possible to allow her time to escape. Then, he was supposed to leave through the front door once it was safe and meet her at the end of the street. She had no time to pause and see, however, because while the crowd still held the agent at bay, they wouldn't be able to do it forever. And they wouldn't have long before reinforcements arrived; Nikki had no doubt Miller had called in Linstead as soon as the group assembled.

"Thank you," she said over her shoulder to the five brave men who'd rushed at an armed FBI agent. "Thank you," she repeated to the other people standing around on the steps as she descended. "Thank you," she reiterated to the press of human beings who watched her as she passed by, opening up to let her through and then closing in around her. Protecting her. What else did you say to those who were prepared to come to a stranger's aid?

"He's okay," Reshma said, waving at the tattooed guy on the deck. "He got tasered, but he's a big, strong man, no worries. He'll be fine." Nikki grimaced and wondered if that was who she'd heard screaming when they'd originally rushed up the steps. The agent would've fired his taser, hitting the first big man in line, but had no hope of stopping five strapping blokes intent on bringing him down. No wonder Tattoo Guy was dark on him.

Now that the crowd had stopped chanting and become almost silent, she could hear the other agent raging and shouting. He was getting closer, even though everyone tried to hold him back.

"We need to hurry," Reshma said, grabbing Nikki's hand and pulling her forward. She led Nikki toward the side fence, away from the driveway and the advancing operative, talking quickly as she did so. "Russell told me everything," Reshma explained. "He made sure all of us at the institute were well-informed. He didn't want anyone to be here who wasn't fully committed. He knew how high the stakes were tonight, even if some of us failed to appreciate it at first. And let me tell you, that man is a very magnificent speaker when he wants to be. He convinced every single employee to come to your aid."

They made it to the fence, and Nikki paused for a second. "I will thank him profusely as soon as I see him," she agreed. "I just wish I could thank everyone else here personally as well."

"The best thanks you can give him, and the rest of us, is to get out of here. Take that dreadful company down. We need some kind of recompense for Tammy and Antoine, and you are going to get that for us." Reshma had tears in her eyes as she spoke, and Nikki also felt teary. She couldn't help herself; she drew Reshma into a fierce hug, and in an uncharacteristic show of affection, Reshma hugged her back. "Now go."

Reshma stepped back and motioned for three of the people nearest to help her make a human step, so they could boost Nikki over the fence and into the neighbor's yard.

Nikki gritted her teeth and pulled the backpack on a little tighter. Then she hopped into the waiting hands of her liberators and had cleared the fence before she even had time to say goodbye.

This was Henry Packham's yard. Her elderly neighbor kept it neat as a pin, thank God. Nikki had only been in the backyard a few times over the years, but it remained much as she remembered it, which helped her navigate through the dark as she felt her way to the far side of the house where she knew there was a gate that'd allow her access to the front. And more importantly, out onto the road.

Nikki poked her head over Henry's front gate—the old man was as deaf as a doorknob and was probably sleeping soundly through all this hullabaloo. She hoped he stayed inside and didn't get involved. He was a sweet gentleman, and it'd just confuse him. She checked out the rest of the street, sending her searching gaze first to her end, then to the other. As Nikki had guessed, quite a few of her neighbors were now standing on their front porches with their lights on, or down by their front gates, watching with curiosity and some trepidation at the kerfuffle going on at her house. The crowd wasn't visible from her vantage point, but she could hear them. There was a lot of incoherent shouting, and someone was even banging a drum. A great diversion to keep the agent's attention centered on them.

There was no sign of Jacob, and her heart squeezed tight. It seemed he hadn't been able to slip past Miller and Bakshi. Yet, she reminded herself. But he would make it. Jacob was smart and well-trained. He would succeed, she had to trust in that.

She wasn't sure she could take the next step if he wasn't by her side.

She might have no choice, however. He'd made her promise she would go without him if he wasn't at the rendezvous on time.

And she needed to go. While there was still a chance, while the agents were still overrun with Russell's cohort of the faithful. Henry's fence was a low iron railing, not so much meant to keep people out as to delineate his property. She pushed her way between two shrubs and stepped neatly over the railing. Now she was standing on the pathway, out in the open, and she felt terribly exposed. Hiking the backpack higher on her shoulders, she turned and jogged down the path toward the other end of the street, away from her house, ignoring her neighbors; they wouldn't recognize her in the darkened street, anyway.

Russell should be waiting in his little blue Mazda at the end of the block. She squinted her eyes. Was that a hint of blue underneath a streetlamp, right down at the intersection behind that large tree trunk? It was still a few hundred yards away, but as she picked up her pace, the car crept forward, so that its nose peeked out onto her street.

It was Russell; it had to be. She surged forward, excitement and adrenaline driving her on. As she got closer, the passenger door swung open, and she could see Russell in the driver's seat beckoning her onward.

She gave a quick glance over her shoulder, hoping to spot Jacob coming up behind. But the street remained empty. She slowed, wondering if she should turn around, go back for him.

"Nikki, come on," Russell yelled. His car was now only fifty yards away.

She was almost safe.

But she didn't want to go without Jacob.

There was a shout, and she turned to see a figure sprinting

down the pathway. It had to be Jacob, although it was hard to be sure as he flashed from dark to light and dark again, passing each streetlamp and on to the next. He was still a long way behind her, but he was waving his hands at her, urging her to run, miming that he would catch up.

With a grin of relief, she jogged over to the car and leaned in the open door.

"Hi, boss." She gave him what she hoped was a cheeky smile. But her relief faded when she caught his gaze and found it fixed on something behind her. Russell's brow furrowed with concern, and she spun around to find out what had worried him.

Jacob had stopped and pivoted, his feet planted akimbo, arms braced by his side.

Turned to face someone running after him.

It took Nikki a few seconds to make out that the dim figure was Agent Miller, charging down the road at full tilt, her gun raised, yelling at the top of her lungs. But she wasn't screaming at Jacob; she was looking past Jacob and shouting Nikki's name, telling her to halt, or she'd shoot.

Nikki could only stand and stare, as frozen as a statue.

Jacob took off like a sprinter starting a race, straight for the agent barreling toward her.

"No!" Nikki screamed.

"Get in the car," Russell demanded, but Nikki remained standing in the open door, watching Jacob run directly into danger, watching Miller point her gun at him.

A hand clamped around her elbow and pulled hard, dragging her forcefully into the car, so that she banged her head on the doorjamb as her butt landed in the seat.

"No," she shouted again. "No, we can't leave him."

"I'm sorry, Nikki," Russell said, his voice grim, but Nikki didn't have time to turn and look at him; still captured by the scene unfolding down the street.

Miller tried to dodge out of Jacob's way, aiming the gun over his shoulder and straight at Nikki. Jacob sidestepped, putting himself directly in the agent's line of fire yet again. What was he doing? Now wasn't the moment to play the hero. He could get hurt. Or killed.

In the background, Nikki noticed a group of people spill out of her driveway and jog down the street toward her.

Jacob had almost reached Miller now. She zigzagged to the other side of the road to avoid him, and he stumbled and half-fell as he changed direction to stop her. Miller was past him now. But then he was on his feet and chasing after her. Miller was fast. But Jacob was faster. He tackled her while they were both running full pelt, and they came to ground in a tumble of arms and legs.

More people were flowing out of her house, all of them now charging down the road toward the agent and Jacob, who were wrestling, rolling over and over on the street.

There was an unmistakable sound of a gunshot, so loud in the quiet street it made Nikki flinch and cover her ears. But just as quickly, she lifted her head and stared down the street. Who had been shot? She couldn't take her eyes off the pair, both lying unmoving in the middle of the road, lit by a puddle of yellow light from a lamp above them. She went to put one foot out of the car, but Russell leaned across her and slammed the door shut. Then he put it into gear and gunned it down the street without a backward glance.

"No, Russell, you have to stop. We have to see if Jacob's okay."

"My job is to get you onto the video link in time for your testimony. This is what Jacob would've wanted. He wouldn't have wanted you to put all of this," Russell waved his hand in the air, indicating the rear vision mirror, "in jeopardy because of him. You are the key, Nikki; you need to remember that."

"No," sobbed Nikki. "No, no." Her heart shattered into a thousand pieces. She curled into the fetal position in the passenger seat and sobbed like a hysterical child.

Sobbed because Jacob might be lying there hurt and she couldn't help him.

Sobbed because he might even die.

Sobbed because she should've told him how she felt about him. She was in love with him.

Sobbed because Russell was right.

But he didn't know one vital detail.

She couldn't do this without Jacob.

CHAPTER SIXTEEN

Jacob wriggled a little lower on the hospital bed, trying to get comfortable against the pile of pillows behind him, but to no avail. His leg ached with a dull throb that permeated every single thought, making it hard to concentrate on anything else, and he wondered whether he should reconsider his choice to only take the bare minimum of the drugs the nurse had offered. He'd wanted to stay alert, wanted to be awake when Nikki arrived. But it was after dinner already, and he worried that perhaps she wasn't coming after all.

He wriggled again, the thick bandages around his thigh making it hard to find the right position. A sharp pain shot down to his toes, and he let out a hiss of pain. A surgeon had operated on his leg early this morning, stitching him up and declaring him to be one lucky man. This was the second time he'd been badly injured, and this bullet wound was worse than the knife slash to his arm that he'd received while apprehending a dealer in the back streets of Luleå a few years ago. Ironically, that offender had been aiming to kill him, fueled by a drug-induced haze, and Jacob had been forced to use a taser to subdue the guy. Whereas Miller hadn't been trying to kill him, not really.

He could still see Miller's face in the few seconds after the gunshot had resounded through the quiet street. She'd gone as white as a sheet, her eyes widening in alarm as realization hit her and she saw the blood streaming from the wound in his thigh. She hadn't meant to shoot him; hadn't wanted to shoot him. She'd just been doing her job, and he'd gotten in her way. But she'd never intended to use her weapon. Jacob had dragged her to the ground, and they'd wrestled over and over, and the gun had gone off accidentally. They'd both just been doing their jobs. Hers had been to stop him at all costs. His had been to protect Nikki at all costs. He'd already accepted that fate. And he'd do it again in a heartbeat. Because he'd kept his promise; he'd protected Nikki, no matter what. He hadn't failed her, like he had Tristan.

"It's OK," he'd told her, even as he'd stifled a scream when she'd rolled him over in the middle of the road and applied pressure to his wound, yelling for someone to call an ambulance.

But he knew it wasn't okay, not for her. She'd failed; had let one of her detainees escape and wounded the other. A terrible result for her and for the FBI. She may lose her job over this, and even if she didn't, he could just imagine the kinds of disciplinary measures they might apply, the amount of paperwork and red tape she'd have to wade through. Especially if Nikki had carried out her task. He was still waiting to hear the outcome of whether her video linkup had even worked. And if it had, had her testimony made any difference?

Miller had hovered beside the ambulance as they'd loaded him in, watching him with haunted eyes. At the last second, she'd reached out and grabbed his hand tight, and said, "I'm sorry. For everything."

"I know," he'd replied. She was a smart lady and was probably just coming to realize the extent of the mission she'd been duped into, wondering if she should've done something differently. It was a shame. He liked Miller and would've been glad to work alongside her any day of the week if only things had been different.

Jacob had been reunited with his cell phone after he'd recovered from surgery, and Mårten had called him an hour ago. It'd been so good to hear his voice; Mårten had been worried sick at Jacob's lack of communication over the past week and a half, and had even been considering booking a ticket over to the US to come find him. Jacob knew that Mårten's worry would be because he felt responsible, since he'd actively participated in Jacob's hair-brained scheme to bring him his passport so he could board that aircraft.

His partner's first concern had been about Jacob's physical state, but Jacob had assured him the bullet had penetrated his upper thigh, missing the bone and vital arteries, and while it was painful and would require a few months of rehab, that he would be fighting fit again soon. Once he'd reassured Mårten, Jacob had to cajole him into revealing how his bosses were feeling about his disappearance back in Sweden. Begrudgingly, Mårten had told him that Rydberg was fuming about Jacob's wild and reckless behavior, and could barely believe he had the audacity to smuggle himself aboard a US military aircraft and then get caught up in some dodgy FBI operation. Jacob could hear in Mårten's voice that he was deeply disturbed by the repercussions Jacob might face once he returned home. Mårten was yet to hear what the deputy commissioner thought about Jacob's vanishing act, as he'd headed back to Västernorrland main headquarters down in Sundsvall. But it took little imagination to know that he would be coldly furious, to say the least. It would reflect badly on him that the officer he'd hand-picked for this mission had gone rogue. It was probably the justification Runar Staaf needed to get rid of Jacob from the force once and for all.

Jacob had been expecting nothing less, but his heart still sank as Mårten confirmed his worst fears. He talked for a few more minutes with Mårten, hoping to reassure him he would be back in Sweden soon, once they cleared him to fly, and then he could defend his actions. But after the phone call ended, he was left wondering if Chief Rydberg was going to be ordered to sack him when he got home, no matter what Jacob said. Which was possibly why Mårten was sounding so jittery; Mårten didn't want to lose Jacob as a partner. And Jacob didn't want to jeopardize that partnership either. But he'd always known getting on that flight might be a one-way ticket. He'd accepted that risk, and now he may well have to live with his decision.

Maybe he needed to become more proactive about the whole thing. If he was going to be sacked anyway, maybe he should quit while he was ahead. Stay in Seattle. A few ideas had been floating around in his head over the past few days, and all of them centered on a petite blonde with the biggest, most beautiful blue eyes he'd ever seen. Centered on how she made him feel, and how quickly he'd come to realize that he didn't want to live a life without her in it.

But then… Well, that's when things became blurry. It seemed unlikely that the Seattle police would take him on if he were dishonorably discharged from the Swedish force. And he didn't know what he would do if he couldn't be a cop. A few vague options tumbled around in his head, but none of them appeared likely to come to fruition. Which left him with the question: would he be happy with a normal nine-to-five job just so he could be with Nikki?

Before he could answer that, however, the door to his room opened and three men stepped in, shutting it silently behind them. Jacob went to sit up higher in the bed then winced as pain speared through him. One man peeled away to the right, positioning himself to the side of the window, giving him a view of the entire front of the building and the parking lot below, which he slowly perused. The second put his back to the door and stood at attention, his eyes never leaving Jacob's face. Which left the third, a tall man with a sharp beak of a nose and an even sharper gaze, who came to stand at the end of Jacob's bed.

No one spoke. But Jacob didn't need to ask; he already knew who these guys were. The FBI. Only this time they were the real deal.

"Mr. Utsi," the guy at the end of his bed said in a clipped tone with a slight accent Jacob couldn't place. "Or should I say, Police Inspector Utsi?" He tilted his head to the side and considered Jacob.

Faan. He knew they'd figure it out eventually. Jacob kept his mouth firmly shut.

The man took his silence as answer enough and went on. "I am Ronald Studebäcker. The director of the FBI." Jacob should've recognized that accent. With a name like that, this man had German heritage. "I want to personally apologize to you. We have it on good authority that Dr. Winter shall be here soon, but I can't stay so I hope you will pass on my apologies to her from me."

Jacob inclined his head slowly, not trusting himself to speak. There were so many warring emotions going on inside his chest that he didn't know which one to dissect first. Uppermost was anger—he wanted to give this fellow a piece of his mind. Next was disappointment; this director had so little control over his own agents he'd allowed possible corruption to stain his agency. He was also somewhat wary; was he about to land in a deep pile of shit? The FBI probably had the power to make him disappear if they wanted to. If they decided to cover this whole thing up so that he and Nikki couldn't cause a scandal, then there was nothing he could do about it. But he took it as a good sign that this man had acknowledged Nikki's existence and told him she was on her way, so perhaps they would be safe after all. And lastly… well…okay, maybe he was also a little in awe. This was the actual director of the FBI, come to apologize in person. The idea was freaking him out.

He already knew Nikki was en route—she'd phoned him using Russell's cell—but he wished she were here to see this. It might go some way to compensate for everything they'd been through. He couldn't wait to hear how the director justified his team's actions. How was he going to explain away what'd happened to Nikki and himself?

"I have only been informed of Supervisory Special Agent Linstead team's…behavior, in the past few hours." The Director tapped a finger distractedly on the small table at the end of the hospital bed, perhaps the only sign that he might be unsettled by what he had to say. "I was under the impression that Linstead and his team were on protection duty, keeping you safe from a direct and immediate threat."

Which was only half right, Jacob thought. But he merely lifted his chin, indicating that Studebäcker should continue.

"What I didn't realize was that Linstead had an ulterior motive. Linstead asked for this mission personally, which perhaps should've raised a red flag. But at the time no one bothered to question him." Studebäcker looked out the window for a second before collecting himself. "He was supposed to keep Dr. Winter under house guard and make sure she remained safe so that he could then escort her to the Supreme Court in Oslo to testify. The first I heard that this hadn't occurred was when the media reported a hundred or so people had converged on your home and shots were fired in the street." Studebäcker focused his intense gaze on Jacob, and Jacob wondered how it must've felt, those initial few seconds when the director knew something had gone terribly wrong with one of his operations. Had his stomach tied in knots and had he slammed his fist down on his deck in anger? Nothing showed on the director's expressionless face, however, and Jacob was left to admire the man's steely reserve.

"I'm very sorry you were hurt. The doctors tell me you will recover given time, and for that I'm extremely glad. But I want to reiterate, Linstead was working outside of our normal parameters, and his team were not privy to that fact. They were just following his orders, and they thought this was another ordinary mission."

Hmm, that was as Jacob had suspected, but it still didn't give him half the answers he needed. He knew the squad would've just been obeying commands, but he also thought that Miller had a hunch something was off as well. Perhaps not enough of a hunch to question Linstead's authority, but given enough time she might have come to her senses. "What's going to happen to Linstead?" Jacob asked.

"I can't tell you specifics." The director continued to stare blandly at Jacob. "There will be disciplinary action."

"Can you give me any sign as to why he was *'working outside the normal parameters'* then?"

The director paused, pursing his lips. "This doesn't leave the room," he said finally. "You're a cop, I'm sure you understand what it means when I tell you that something is off the record."

Jacob nodded and leaned forward.

"Linstead has an uncle who is a state senator. I won't reveal which state. This senator has a vested interest in seeing that the Chinese fish company does not lose its farming lease. Needless to say, we will investigate him for fraud, collusion and maybe even treason, among other things."

Jacob leaned back against his pillow. Wow, okay, that was unexpected. But perhaps not as shocking as the director might imagine. Jacob and Nikki had discussed the many options for the driving force behind her testimony being blocked by the FBI, and extortion or bribery by an outside party had definitely been one scenario on the table. Jacob opened his mouth to ask for more details on this shady senator, like was he also linked to the attempt on Nikki's life and the murder of her two colleagues? And was he the one who'd ordered the assassinations? But knew it would be futile. The director had given him all the information he was prepared to pass on right now.

Instead, he said, "Can I ask a personal favor?"

Studebäcker raised a single eyebrow in inquiry.

"That you are lenient with Agent Miller?" The director lowered his eyebrows, but said nothing. "She was the only person with any integrity in this whole debacle," Jacob continued. "She was following orders from a senior officer who she had no cause to doubt. I believe she trusted she was carrying out a sanctioned mission, and I don't think she should be punished for that." As were all the other agents, but then he hadn't got to know them at all and so didn't feel he needed to ask for clemency for them as well.

"I'll take your comments under review," the director replied after a moment's contemplation. "But I also need to consider that she let a hoard of unarmed private citizens overpower her, failed to keep a witness under her protection from escaping, and then discharged her weapon, wounding an innocent man. None of those things are up to the standards our agents have a sworn duty to uphold."

Jacob blew out a breath. When Studebäcker put it like that, it didn't look good for Miller. "She's a good agent," Jacob said, hoping the director would take his assessment into account.

"Get well soon, Inspector Utsi." The director turned on his heel, and the three men disappeared out of the room as quickly and silently as they'd entered. Jacob dropped his shoulders as he eased back into the pillow, his mind spinning with all the permutations of what Studebäcker had revealed. He wondered about the ramifications of everything that'd gone down. The mere fact that the director of the FBI had paid him a personal visit suggested just how much in the shit the agency might be.

At least it answered one question. The reason they hadn't been taken to a safe house when they'd first arrived in Seattle was now clear. Linstead would've been able to keep his mission directives within the confines of his small team that way. If they'd used a safe house, there would've been a high possibility of Linstead's antics getting back to his superiors, and someone might conceivably have stopped him.

A nurse came in ten minutes later to check his vitals, breaking him out of his spiraling thoughts. This time Jacob accepted her offer of stronger drugs, but only after she effectively called him an idiot for trying to be a hero and tough it out when she realized his pain levels were increasing. She was probably right, and he could hear a trace of Nikki's tone in the nurse's gruff voice, and knew she would've said the same thing.

Where was Nikki? Why was she taking so long? He missed her; he needed her here beside him, just to know that she was unharmed, and whole. And his. It didn't shock him as much as it should have to realize how much he needed her. It was as if she carried the missing piece of his heart that he'd never been aware was absent until now.

The nurse departed, leaving him alone, restless, and a little desperate.

The drugs took effect, and he could feel his eyelids getting heavy. No, he needed to stay awake; she was coming. He shook his head, hoping to clear it, and then suddenly, there she was, standing at the foot of his bed like an angel descended from heaven. He hadn't even heard her come in.

Russell poked his head around the door, gave a quick thumbs up and then retreated, but Jacob barely registered his presence; he only had eyes for Nikki.

"Jacob, I've been so worried. Is your leg...?" Her eyes filled with tears as she studied the thick bandages covering his thigh.

"I'm okay. Come here." He opened his arms, and she rushed to him, kissing him hard on the mouth before burying her face in his neck, but keeping away from his injured side. They stayed like that for moments uncounted as Jacob drew her in; her warmth, her physical presence, her smell, the feel of her slim shoulders beneath his palms, her rapidly beating heart, which was slowing to a more normal rate as he held her. She was here, and she was fine. And now he would be fine too.

At last she lifted her head, scrubbing at her wet cheeks, pulling back so she could look him in the eye. "Russell kept telling me you were okay, but I had to see for myself. I can't believe you did that. You tackled an armed FBI agent to the ground."

By way of an answer, he used his thumb to lightly brush away the last of her tears, savoring the feel of her soft skin along her high cheekbones, staring into the blue depths of her eyes.

"I was protecting you," he replied.

She looked at him long and hard, and he could practically hear the cogs whirring inside her brain as she debated how to answer him. Was she going to be angry because he'd risked everything for her? Or was she feeling guilty that she'd got away unscathed because he'd put his life on the line for her? Or was she sad, regretting that he'd been wounded and that their perfect escape plan hadn't worked out so perfectly in the end?

He thought he saw all of those emotions and more flit over

her face, but eventually, she said, "Thank you," and he grinned, grateful that she'd chosen to honor his sacrifice, instead of condemn him, as she so easily could have. He was sure she'd have plenty more to say on the topic; he could read it behind her eyes, but for now they were both alive and in one piece, and that was all that mattered.

"How did you go? Did you manage to testify?" he queried. Because this was the crux of the whole thing. If the video link had failed, or the defense lawyers on the other end hadn't asked the right questions, this could all have been for nothing. The plan had been for Russell to take Nikki back to his house so she could use his reliable Wi-Fi and where they were hopefully safe for however long it took to talk to the court.

She nodded. "Yes, it all worked like a dream. Russell already had his computer and everything set up, so all we had to do when we got to his house was log in. But oh, gosh, Jacob, I could barely think. Barely even speak. I was so worried about what'd happened to you. That poor judge must've thought I was an imbecile, not a world-renowned specialist." She gave a wan smile.

He nodded sympathetically. "But you got it out in the end?"

Nikki straightened from where she'd been bending over the bed to hug him, but she didn't let go of his hand. "Yes, the chief lawyer asked for a short recess when I first logged on— he could see I was rattled, but he didn't know why—and Russell read me the riot act, so I finally pulled myself together." Nikki grimaced, although Jacob found it hard to imagine the mild-mannered, bohemian Russell that Nikki had described raising his voice to anyone. "After that, I was on the virtual stand for three hours. The prosecution tried to discredit me, of course, but the lawyers on our side kept objecting or coming back to me to clarify my answers. In the end, the prosecution ran out of avenues to pursue. After all, our research speaks for itself. You can't argue with facts and figures." He knew the world wasn't that black and white, but Nikki was a scientist through and through, and as such, she believed unequivocally that the facts never lied. He loved that her blue eyes were now sparking with heat and resolution, the same stubborn strength of character she'd showed on the very first day, when she'd stood up to him in the little hut in the snow, demanding to know what was going on.

"Russell had already warned me that the lawyers on both sides had been banned from mentioning why I was giving my testimony via video. You see, the murders and the attempt on my life are all just allegations at the moment, and until they prove the gunmen who killed Tammy and Antoine were hired by Diàoyú, then it's inadmissible in court. But the judge seemed to know something dodgy was going on, he asked a few pointed questions why I had suddenly replaced Tammy as the specialist, and when the lawyer told him that Tammy had died in tragic circumstances and there was now an ongoing criminal investigation, the judge looked most interested."

"Hmm. That's a good thing," Jacob replied, smothering a large yawn. At least the judge suspects Diàoyú of foul play, even if he can't take it into account when he makes his ruling.

"I guess so." Nikki bit her bottom lip, her gaze drifting to the window where the lights of Seattle flickered outside. "Russell and I waited until the end of the court session, just in case they wanted to recall me, which was mid-morning, our time. But Russell wouldn't let me come and see you until he'd contacted the FBI and had assurances there would not be any repercussions for me. That I was a free woman."

"Great." Now that the first hit of dopamine from having Nikki back in his arms was fading, he could feel the drugs taking effect. His body was becoming heavy and lethargic, his mind sluggish, and he was finding it hard to focus on her words.

"I'm sorry," he muttered, rubbing his eyes. "They doped me up with meds for the pain, and now I'm feeling a little woozy." He tried to fight it, shaking his head and squeezing his eyes shut before popping them open again, but the fog continued to creep in around the edges.

"I should leave you to get some sleep."

"No, stay. I'll sleep better with you in my arms."

"What about your leg?"

"With you by my side, I'm feeling no pain." He looked up imploringly at her. His eyelids felt so heavy they could've been weighed down with concrete. But he would not succumb, not until she said she'd stay in his arms. The drugs might be numbing the pain, but they were also numbing his ability to think and even speak. He wondered vaguely if the nurse had slipped a sedative in among the other medications.

"Okay," she agreed, then she sat gingerly on the bed and swung her legs up so that she was lying above the covers on his uninjured side. "Are you sure this isn't hurting you?"

"Babe, I'm in heaven right now," he sighed, tucking her shoulder underneath his arm so she could lay her head on his chest. "This is exactly where I'm meant to be. I couldn't ask for any place better." At last, he gave in to the cotton wool crowding his brain and the lethargy that caused his body to feel like it was made of lead and let his eyes close. He knew he could sleep soundly tonight, as long as he had Nikki safe and warm in his arms.

CHAPTER SEVENTEEN

Nikki awoke with a start. It took her a few seconds to orient herself, but at last she remembered she was lying in a hospital bed next to Jacob, and relaxed. She had no idea what time it was, but it must be in the wee hours of the morning, as the building was quiet and dim. Jacob slept on, oblivious, alongside her, for which she was grateful. He needed to heal, and rest was the best antidote to his pain.

She could still scarcely breathe when she thought about watching him prostrate in the middle of the road as Russell drove her away, powerless to help him. She hadn't been lying when she'd told him she could barely form a coherent word during the first part of her testimony; her brain had been focused on only one thing. Him.

There were so many things she wanted to say to Jacob about the stupidity of his act. And about the bravery of his act. Earlier, she'd seen in his eyes that it hadn't been the right time to berate him, to let all her mixed emotions out in one confusing stream. So she'd thanked him for his courage. Because he was a hero. Even if he was a stupid hero. And she knew it meant a lot to him; that he'd kept his promise to protect her at all costs. She could see it in his eyes; it was as if he'd gained back a small part of his honor, a part that'd been misplaced until that moment.

Nikki tilted her head back so she could look up at his face. A small night-light was set above the bed, touching the hospital room with its pale luminescence. In the dim glow, his features in repose had a softer edge, the intensity and toughness he kept up as a façade when he was working as a cop no longer in evidence. Something in her chest constricted at the sight of him. A terribly sweet, but also desolate feeling washed over her.

Her stupid heart wanted things it just couldn't have. But as she traced the ridge of his dark eyebrows with her fingertips, ran it down his aquiline nose and over his firm lips, her need for him became overwhelming. How could she ever let this feeling go? She did not know how or why it'd happened, but over the past week and a half—such a short time—she'd fallen hard for Inspector Jáhkot Utsi.

This man had raced into the face of danger to protect her. He'd taken a bullet for her. He hadn't actually said the words, but his actions screamed that he at the very least cared for her deeply; perhaps he even loved her.

Just as she loved him.

She knew that now. She loved him, without a doubt.

But could she tell him that to his face?

She lifted her head from his shoulder so she could stare more deeply at his profile. If he were awake right now, would she be able to form the words? What if he rejected her, said that he was heading back to Sweden, and while it'd been fun knowing her, he was going to continue with the rest of his life? What if he'd played her for a fool? What if he didn't love her like she thought?

She uttered a small sound of frustration. Not wanting to wake him, she wriggled a little higher on the bed, unable to lie quietly any more. She needed to get up, to move, to pace the floor and work out these unsettling feelings.

Jacob smiled in his sleep and murmured something incomprehensible, wrapping his arm tighter around her waist, and she froze.

Gosh darn it. Now she was trapped. A very nice place to be trapped, she admitted, but her heart felt like it was about to burst out of her chest, and she needed action to release these emotions, or she might just detonate. Trying to calm her racing pulse, she lay still for a few more moments. But it was no good; she had to get out of this bed. Moving as carefully as she could, she eased first one leg off the bed, and then moved her other one, hoping the drugs would keep him asleep even as she lifted his fingers to unclasp them from her hip.

"Hey, watcha doing?" His sleepy voice surprised her, and she nearly banged her head on his chin as she sat up with a start.

"Oh, sorry, I didn't mean to wake you. I was just…a little uncomfortable."

"Are you trying to tell me that sleeping in my arms all night isn't the nicest thing you've ever done?" His brow furrowed in concern as he looked up at her.

"No, no…it's not that at all."

A deep laugh reverberated through his chest as his lips twitched up.

He was kidding. Of course he was. Her mind was so muddled that she couldn't see it at first. That was all.

"Sorry," she said again, unable to think of the right thing to say. Some of her consternation must've shown on her face, however, because the frown came back, a real one this time.

"What's the matter? You seem a little rattled. Did you have a bad dream?"

"No. No bad dream. I just couldn't sleep."

Jacob's scowl deepened, and he let go of her so he could lever himself higher in the bed, eliciting a sharp intake of breath as he moved his injured leg. Now she'd done it. She hadn't wanted to wake him, and not only was he now wide awake, but he was in pain because of her.

"Tell me what's going on," he demanded. "I can see it in your eyes, Nikki, you're frightened. But of what?"

Was she scared? Perhaps she was. But not from any physical threat. This fear sprang from a well deep inside her. The fear of rejection. The fear of being left alone. Of the way he made her feel. And of never feeling like this ever again.

"I was just thinking…" She gulped and got off the bed, no longer able to sit still and stare into his eyes. At least this way, if he rejected her, she wouldn't have to endure the excruciating pain of having to watch his eyes turn to shadow, slowly shutting her out. Jacob grabbed her hand at the last moment, anchoring her to his bedside, but she still refused to look at him.

"You were thinking?" he prompted.

"Umm, yes. I was thinking…wondering, really…what's going to happen after…you know…after you get out of the hospital. I guess you have to go back to Sweden, but…"

"Nikki, look at me."

It took all her courage, but she raised her gaze until she met his.

"You know I have American citizenship, don't you?"

"Of course, I remember." Nikki gulped some air, afraid even to think the words, let alone say them. Was he implying what she thought he was implying?

"So I can stay here as long as I like."

"Hmm," she answered with a noncommittal hum. Did that mean he *was* going to stay?

"And I could even get a job here if I wanted. Because I think I may need a new one after my boss is finished with me." He drew her toward him until she was close enough to lay his palm along the side of her face. She wanted to melt into his touch.

"But I guess there would be only one true reason to stick around. And that would be for you. Do you want me to stay, Nikki?"

Did she want him to? Oh, gosh, yes.

Could she tell him that? To his face?

Calling on all her strength buried deep inside, she stared into his eyes. Warm and brown and compassionate. The awareness made her catch her breath. He knew. He knew how she felt about him. But he waited patiently. Waited for her to say the words.

"With all my heart," she whispered, letting herself drown in those whisky-colored eyes. "I know this might be crazy, because I was never one to believe in love at first sight, but I've fallen in love with you." Her heart was pounding so hard against the inside of her ribcage, she was sure it was going to burst out of her body.

"We both must be a little crazy then," he replied softly. "Because I never believed in love at first sight either. Until I met you." Now her heart felt like it'd flown right out of her chest and was soaring high above them. So this was what pure happiness felt like. A feeling so strong it may destroy her. Burn her, cleanse her from the inside out, until there was nothing left but joy and yearning.

"So, you'll stay?" She could barely believe it might be true.

"I think we should give this thing a chance. Don't you?"

"Yes." She clambered onto the bed, carefully straddling his hips, her lips fusing with his, her fingers running through the short hair at the nape of his neck. "Yes, yes, yes," she breathed as she buried her face in his collarbone, drawing in the scent of him, feeling his powerful shoulders beneath her palms.

She lifted her head and stared into his eyes. This man was everything. They would make this work. She hadn't said it, but even if she had to move to Sweden to be with him, she knew she would do so in a heartbeat. Her job was important to her; it was part of who she was and what she believed in. Her passion for preserving the wild places on this planet would always rule her heart and drive her onward. And she loved working at the Institute, but she would find another job if need be. Jacob was worth it. Love was worth it.

CHAPTER EIGHTEEN

THREE MONTHS LATER

Nikki was lost in thought, kneeling on the ground and staring at the gravestone as if it might somehow give her the answers she needed. She made sure to come and visit Tammy's grave every week, sometimes sitting for an hour or more, looking at the marble and wishing things could've been different. Nikki had also been to visit Clark, Tammy's husband, in the weeks after the funeral, and although that meeting had been heart wrenching, it'd offered Nikki a strange comfort, and perhaps Clark as well. But, how she missed her friend. A single tear rolled down her cheek. Gosh darn it, she'd promised herself she wouldn't cry this time, but she still regretted not being able to attend Tammy or Antoine's funerals. Perhaps if she had, then she would've felt some kind of closure, but as it was, she'd always mourn her friends taken too soon in such a violent manner. What was the world coming to if greed was the driving force behind everything humans did?

Perhaps the only silver lining from Tammy's death was how all the staff at the Institute had come together. Everyone had been shocked to hear of Tammy and Antoine's deaths, and at first they had milled around in the corridors, speaking in outraged tones, but unsure what they could do to redress the situation. Then, Russell Morgan had rallied them all, asking for their support to help free Nikki and Jacob, and every single one of them had answered the call, hoping to right a wrong. No one wanted this to happen again to another hard-working scientist who was only doing his or her job. And so they had all come to fight the tyranny of injustice, and it'd touched Nikki's heart forever.

Around a month after Russell's rent-a-crowd had freed her from the FBI, Nikki held a huge *thank you* party in her backyard. She went around and expressed her gratitude to every single person who had turned up that night. But she saved her special thanks for the five big men who had put their own safety at risk and tackled an armed FBI agent on her back porch. And Reshma Siram, of course. The conservation analyst seemed to come out of her shell more these days, now talking openly to other staff in the lunchroom, no longer hiding in her office, and she had made quite a few new friends in the past few months, Nikki being one of them. Nikki found Reshma had a wicked sense of humor, to go along with her intelligent mind and demure personality, and she wondered why she'd never noticed it before.

Russell had started a new trend, a monthly morning tea held in the main auditorium so that there was room for everyone to attend. It wasn't compulsory, but he asked that they try to find the time to come, so they could gather in memory of Tammy and Antoine. It was a lovely method of bringing people together, and Nikki had noticed many folks from different sections beginning to talk to others they would never normally have dealings with. Russell was opening the channels of communication, and Nikki hoped things would stay that way. Russell had also recently established a scholarship in Tammy's name at Seattle University, for two students per year to be fully paid to study environmental science with a major in marine science. It would by no means bring Tammy back, but at least her legacy would continue, hopefully for a long time to come.

"You okay, babe?" A warm hand landed on her shoulder.

Jacob's touch shook her out of her thoughts, and she welcomed his gentle contact. He always insisted on coming with her when she visited the cemetery, walking her up to the gravesite, but then leaving her in solitude to contemplate her friend in peace. He remained unobtrusively by the car, but she knew he watched her like a hawk.

Jacob's protective instincts remained on high alert, even though the Swedish police had captured the two gunmen who'd tried to kill her. The FBI were still struggling to figure who was responsible for giving the order to murder two scientists in cold blood and make an attempt on a third—it seemed likely it was some high up official in the Chinese fish company, but Diàoyú was stonewalling them, and the Chinese government were doing nothing to force the issue. With no authority in China, the FBI could do only continue to appeal to the Chinese government to allow them access to the company. From the little Studebäcker would reveal in his two short phone calls to Jacob while he was recovering in hospital, the unnamed state senator had no knowledge of the assassins hired to kill Nikki, his role had been to stop Nikki from testifying, not to kill her. So, they may never find the culprit. Even though the hitmen would spend the rest of their lives in a Swedish jail, the true killer had got away with murder and would remain free, perhaps forever.

The one consolation to all the death and greed, however, was that two months ago the judge had passed his ruling on the Diàoyú case. After only half a day of deliberation, the judge had declared that the Chinese company had broken most, if not all the regulations laid down by the Norwegian government to protect the fjords, and ordered them to halt trading immediately and dismantle every single fish farm. It'd been a huge win for the environment, and Nikki had cried when she'd heard the result. The lawyers told her that her testimony played a large role in the judge's decision. It'd never bring back her friends, but at least Nikki felt some vindication for everything she'd been through. It'd all been worth it to stop that greedy, callous company from raping and pillaging the pristine marine habitats anymore.

Nikki lifted her chin to look at Jacob and gave him her hand so he could help her up. "Yes, sorry. I'm still so mad, that's all." She got to her feet. Winter was fading to spring here in Seattle, but that wind had razor-sharp icicles for teeth.

"I know. So am I." He pulled her into his embrace, and she drew warmth and strength from within his arms. She didn't blame Jacob for his overprotectiveness; she continued to jump at every loud noise and constantly checked that her doors and windows were locked. It was just human nature to remain on edge after the terrifying things they'd seen and done. Perhaps they should both see a counselor before this skittishness became a habit they couldn't break.

Nikki pulled back from Jacob's embrace so she could glance at her phone to check the time. "Oh, gosh, you're going to be late for your meeting. Quick, let's go." She'd been mulling over Tammy's grave for longer than she realized.

"I'm sure Studebäcker will wait. He was the one who contacted me, after all," Jacob replied with a wry smile. The director of the FBI had called Jacob out of the blue a few days ago, saying that he'd be in town on business and requesting a meeting. Jacob was pretty sure the man intended to offer him a job. He had it on good authority—from Mårten, who'd told him Chief Superintendent Rydberg was dropping not-so-subtle hints that the FBI had been in touch and were possibly headhunting Jacob—but she knew he was going to play it cool, nonetheless.

Jacob tucked her under his arm, and they ambled back to her car.

"Will you take the job if he offers it to you?"

"Don't know yet?" Jacob replied. "Depends on what he proposes. There'd be lots of training involved if I were to become an actual FBI agent. And that might mean time away from you." He glanced down at her. "I'm not sure I'm up for that."

She wasn't sure she was up for it either. This fledgling romance was stronger than even they'd both dreamed it could be, but it was still in that honeymoon phase where neither could bear to let the other out of their sight for long. New recruits had to endure a rigorous five-month training regime at the FBI Academy in Quantico before they were allowed into the service, which was too long to be apart.

There was also the problem of Jacob's bullet wound. His leg was still healing, and while he could walk with almost no trace of a limp now, it'd be a few more months before he would trust it to chase down a fleeing felon, or attempt a high-intensity training course.

"Maybe he's got something else in mind for you," Nikki surmised. "You were a cop, after all. You already have plenty of skills."

Jacob grimaced at her past-tense use of the word, but said nothing. His trip back to Sweden a few weeks after he was discharged from hospital hadn't been the most pleasant of experiences. It was as he feared. He'd more than overstepped the boundaries of protocol by fleeing the country without permission, and he was already on suspension without pay before he even made it home. If Jacob hadn't quit, he would've most likely faced another inquiry and a possible dishonorable discharge. It didn't make one iota of difference that both Jacob and Mårten had been cleared of any misconduct in the first investigation, on their mission to protect Tristan. The Special Investigations Division would not let Jacob get away with it a second time. Even Biträdande Poliskommissarie Runar Staaf, who'd been the one to set Jacob on this path initially, couldn't shelter him from this giant fuck-up, not that it seemed he wanted to. Jacob had talked to the deputy commissioner on the phone after he quit and the man had thanked him for his service and wished him all the best in his new life in a cold, distant voice; the deputy commissioner had never overcome his dislike of Jacob, and didn't try to hide it.

Chief Rydberg had been less happy about the outcome, but he had to accept Jacob's resignation, because even though he knew Jacob's heart was in the right place and he was a good cop—a great cop, actually—his knack for not following protocol could no longer be overlooked. There were only so many times Rydberg could cover up Jacob's unorthodox ways of getting the job done. So when Rydberg heard the FBI were potentially looking to recruit him, he wasn't afraid to give him a glowing report. Let him become the FBI's problem, Rydberg had joked; perhaps they might be able to pull him into line.

Nikki had accompanied Jacob to Sweden, and after he'd faced the wrath of his commanding officers, they'd traveled together back to Jokkmokk to sort out his life for his move to America. Their first port of call was to see his mother and sister and break the news. His announcement had shocked his mother, Märta, but the Sámi were a stoic race, and she'd smiled and told Jacob that if this is what he truly wanted, then meeting Nikki must be fate. Once Märta had spent a few days in their company and seen him and Nikki together, she softened her view even more. She was overjoyed that Jacob finally seemed happy. And if that meant losing him back to his birth country, then so be it.

They'd also visited Petar, Jacob slapping his old friend on the back and decreeing it was time to trade in that old rust bucket of a Volvo for a newer version. It was his backhanded way of thanking the man for helping to save their lives. Nikki had thanked him in the more traditional method, by wrapping him up in a big hug and kissing him on the cheek, which made Petar blush profusely.

She had loved visiting Sweden a second time; the country was growing on her—it was so beautiful. They had promised to go back to have next Christmas with his family. Perhaps they might return to the little hut by the frozen lake and spend a few days just chilling out in the sauna. Naked. Together. The idea made Nikki smirk to herself. Yes. She would make a booking and surprise Jacob; it could be her Christmas present to him.

They reached her car, and Jacob held the passenger door open for her. "Thank you," she said with a heartfelt smile. Once he was seated next to her in the car, she said, "I think Mårten will be impressed when he comes over to find his ex-partner is now an FBI agent."

Jacob made a scoffing noise. "I don't believe Mårten is that easily impressed."

"Maybe. Maybe not," Nikki replied blithely.

She'd met Mårten in Luleå at the police station, straight after Jacob had handed in his resignation. He'd been waiting for Jacob in the staffroom when he'd come out of Chief Rydberg's office, there to offer moral support if Jacob needed it.

"It's good to finally meet you." Mårten had extended a hand in greeting. Nikki had been a little taken aback as she stared up into his ice-blue eyes. Or were they silver? It was hard to tell. Was it a prerequisite that all Swedish cops be good-looking? Because, aside from Jacob of course, Mårten was one of the most impressive men she'd met. Tall, with lean hips and broad shoulders. There were touches of gray at his temples and forehead in his otherwise dark hair, and the thought *silver fox* flashed across her mind, even though he wouldn't have been old enough to fill that category.

But she wasn't completely blinded by his striking looks, and she got the feeling there was much left unsaid behind Mårten's bland words. That he was perhaps evaluating her, wanting to see what the woman who was taking his police partner away from him was like. She didn't blame him; she and Jacob were moving fast, but she knew deep in her gut they were doing the right thing. So she'd looked him straight in the eye, and said, "Nice to meet you too." But instead of shaking his hand, she reached up and hugged the man. She understood how he felt; he was losing a person dear to him, and she was the one gaining from his loss. She owed him her gratitude.

"I'll make sure he's happy in Seattle, I promise," she'd whispered into his ear, and he'd withdrawn, surprised. But with a look in his eye that implied perhaps he was satisfied with her response.

"Thank you," was his simple reply.

Then Jacob had slapped him on the back, and said, "I told you, man. She's special. Mårten let her go, giving her a careful sideways glance as he did so. It seemed like the jury was still out on that point, but hopefully she could prove herself to him.

She'd followed behind as the two men made their way down the hallway, listening as they bantered back-and-forth.

"You know you've dropped me in the shit, don't you?" Mårten had said. "You'll never guess who Rydberg has partnered me up with now that you're gone."

"Yeah, I heard the rumors," Jacob replied with a grin, bumping Mårten with his shoulder.

"She's a bloody rookie with too much to prove and an

attitude bigger than anyone I know," Mårten had groused.

"Come on, it won't be that bad. Aurora is a good kid, and you're a great cop. You'll be excellent for her; she'll learn a lot from you."

Nikki assumed they meant the young officer she'd met the last time she'd been in the station. The one who rescued her from the hallway and taken her to the lunchroom while Jacob was talking to the deputy commissioner. Aurora had seemed smart and down to earth. Mårten might not like Rydberg's recent choice of partner, but she didn't doubt there was a reason behind the chief's decision, and maybe as Jacob said, Mårten would be good for her.

Mårten had taken them out to lunch as a final farewell, but he'd hinted that he would be over for a visit soon, and Nikki had encouraged him to come. She didn't want Jacob to lose touch with his life in Sweden. If Mårten were to visit, he would see how happy they were together, perhaps putting his mind at ease. And now they had just heard that Mårten had arranged for some leave and would be over to experience an early summer in Seattle.

"Well, I'm looking forward to his visit," she said. "We could all jump on a flight and take him to Las Vegas for the weekend. What do you think?"

"Hmm," he replied noncommittally.

"Oh, come on, I know you're just as excited for his visit as I am," she said, lifting her chin. He wouldn't admit it, but Nikki knew he was a tad nervous about his friend coming. Deep down, Jacob was hoping to get his ex-partner's tick of approval. For his new life and his new love.

"Maybe. Maybe not," Jacob replied with a wry smile, while keeping his eyes on the road ahead.

"Oh, you." She slapped him playfully on the arm. "Fine, stay in denial, but you can't fool me."

As Jacob steered the car toward the city center, Nikki

mulled over the past month's events. "Do you think Studebäcker will have any more news about who was responsible for murdering Tammy and Antoine?"

Jacob shot her a sympathetic look, but shook his head. "You know I'll ask. But you also know that he's told us everything he's allowed to."

"Yeah, yeah. It's all confidential, blah, blah, blah. We're just the poor plebs who nearly lost our lives, yet we get told nothing." She frowned hard at the windshield, tamping down her sudden, building anger. On a certain level, Nikki understood why the FBI were withholding details; a state senator was involved after all. But it still rankled that the person who hired those hitmen, who gave the order to kill Tammy and Antoine, remained at large.

Jacob laid a sympathetic hand on her knee; he felt exactly the same, but he was just more philosophical about it. "I'm sure he'll tell us if he's heard anything new. He's a good man, deep down."

She swallowed the lump in her throat and turned to look at Jacob; he was right, of course. Laying her own hand on top of his, she rubbed her thumb over his knuckles. The feel of his skin on hers soothed her, and the anger leached from her body. The warmth of his palm seeped through her jeans. She loved his hands, the long, strong fingers, the feel of them as he stroked her skin, the clever way he found the sensitive spots and played them until she was left gasping for breath. His grip tightened on her thigh, and a surge of heat shot through her. He had this effect on her, could ignite a spark deep in her belly and turn it into a raging inferno in the space between two breaths. It was devastating, but in a good way. God, she needed him so much. How had she ever lived without him? Her desire for this man was fierce.

"I love you," she said, meaning it with every fiber of her being. Truly, madly, deeply.

"I love you too." Those words alone had the power to give her heart wings. She suddenly wished they weren't in the car. Wished they were back at her cottage, so she could tear his clothes from his body and show him just how much he meant to her. Instead, she smiled at him, hoping she could convey everything she was feeling in her eyes. He smiled back, that gorgeous dimple lighting up his face.

The FBI Seattle Division had an office on 3rd Avenue, and by some miracle, Jacob found a park almost directly in front of the building.

"Will you be okay out here for a while?" he asked.

"Yes." She nodded. Of course she would. They'd already discussed it. She wanted to wait for him, to hear what Studebäcker had to say, and to celebrate with her man when he was offered a position with the FBI.

Jacob reached for the metal water bottle in the center console and took a long swig—no more plastic bottles for him; he was a convert now. His Adam's apple bobbed as he swallowed, and Nikki knew this was perhaps the only sign that he was a tad nervous, despite his protestations.

"Wish me luck," he said, grasping the door handle.

"You don't need luck, Jacob Utsi." She took his hand and drew him toward her for a kiss. "You are the finest, most honorable, most tenacious man I know. They'd be lucky to have *you*." She emphasized the last word, then kissed him again, breathing him in, and letting her certainty flow out through her lips. Letting him know she had faith in him. That she loved him, no matter the outcome. "I'll be waiting," she said simply.

He gave her a cheeky wink and exited the car, but she already knew the result. Knew it in her heart of hearts. She watched his broad shoulders as he crossed the road, so tall and straight, and was so glad he was the one. She now believed in love at first sight, because he was her soulmate.

Their life together would be great. They had a future that would span decades. They'd get married, have children, and grow old together. It was written in the stars. Jacob Utsi had saved Nikita Winter's heart by giving her the courage to trust again. And maybe, just maybe, she'd saved his heart right back.

Also by Suzanne Cass

NEW
Women's Mystery Romance Fiction
Single Title
Finding Kait

Dark Tides Series
Mystery and Romance collide.
Into the Rain
Rain Washed
The Clearing Rain

Stormcloud Station Series
(A Stargazer Spinoff Series)
Small Town Romantic Suspense
Clear Skies
Starlit Skies
Crystal Skies
Dawn Skies
Tangled Skies
Outback Skies

Stargazer Ranch Romance Series
Small Town Romantic Suspense
Combustion: Prequel Novella
Wildfire
Firelight
Snowbound: A Christmas Novella
Snowfall
Cloudburst
Silverstorm

Island Bound Series
Mystery Romance (on an Island)

Books can be read as stand-alone
Bound by Truth
Bound by Silence
Bound by the Stars

Colors of the Earth Series
Small Town Romantic Suspense
Books can be read as stand-alone
Shadows in the Dust
Shadows in Deep Blue
Shadows of Red Earth

Romantic Suspense
Single Title
Island Redemption
Glass Clouds
Chasing Bullets

Love in the Mountains Novella Series
Small Town Short Romance
Novellas can be read as stand-alone
Rain on a Tin Roof
Lost and Found
Rescue his Heart

Please Leave a Review
The greatest gift you could ever give an author is to leave a review. You will be helping other people to discover this book and making a difference to me as an Independently Published Author. If you liked this book and want other people to read it too, please leave a review.

About the Author

Suzanne Cass is an Australian author who writes rural romance and romantic suspense abounding with passion and danger.

Her debut novel, Island Redemption, won the Romance Writers of Australia Emerald Award in 2016. Suzanne was also a finalist in the 2019 Romance Writers of Australia RUBY award.

She had always had a fascination with the tough resilience of people who live in our amazing red-dirt outback country. When not writing about the characters that inhabit her head, Suzanne can be found roaming the Perth beaches with her border collie, or encouraging from the sidelines as her two sons play sport.

Or you can stay in touch via my website
www.suzannecass.com

Or find me on these platforms.

Facebook: www.facebook.com/suzannecassauthor/
Instagram: www.instagram.com/suzanne.cass/
Pintrest: www.pinterest.com.au/suzanne_cass/